PROJECT DEATH
A Tito Rico Mystery

by

Richard Bertematti

Arte Público Press
Houston, Texas
1997

This volume is made possible through grants from the National Endowment for the Arts (a federal agency), Andrew W. Mellon Foundation, the Lila Wallace-Reader's Digest Fund and the City of Houston through The Cultural Arts Council of Houston, Harris County.

Recovering the past, creating the future

Arte Público Press
University of Houston
Houston, Texas 77204-2090

Cover illustration and design by Vega Design Group

Bertematti, Richard.
      Project death : a Tito Rico mystery /
      by Richard Bertematti.
         p.   cm.
      ISBN 1-55885-193-3 (clothbound : alk. paper)
      I. Title.
      PS3552.E7734P76   1997
      813'.54—DC21   96-49346
                                      CIP

PROJECT DEATH

A Tito Rico Mystery

CHAPTER ONE

A black guy wearing a leather cap wanted to sell me a gold chain for fifteen dollars just as I was ready to cut into the projects through a broken metal fence. He was insistent, and followed me all the way to Pepito's building, begging me to buy the chain. He got too close to me, dangling the chain in front of my face with a dirty hand, and I thought of pegging him in the mouth for bothering me. By the time he split because he saw the police and the ambulances, he only wanted five dollars for it.

My friend Pepito lived near 125th, in the Sherman projects stretching from Broadway to Morningside Avenue. The projects were composed of ten massive red-brick buildings, filling two whole blocks, with glass-littered playgrounds, grassy spaces, and walking paths in between the buildings. I couldn't imagine how many people lived in the projects. Thousands. All packed in as little space as possible. The projects were built tough. Everything was bolted down. What wasn't made of concrete was made of steel, unbreakable and cold. There was no nonsense about living in the projects, no fineries and pleasantries. You decorated your apartment any way you wanted, but once you stepped into the hallway, you were on common, and dangerous, ground. Only graffiti added any aesthetic sense to the projects. But that was true only of the seventies, when I was growing up, when the kids were artists. Today they scribble their tags and other nonsense as if they were in a hurry.

It all started that Saturday morning when Pepito came to see me just as I was ready to fry some eggs. I usually knew his knock. But that time he beat my door as if he was angry with it. When I opened the door, he came in fast and slammed the door behind him.

"¿*Qué pasa*, Pepito?" I asked. "What's da mattah wit'ju?"

Pepito was a foot shorter than me and so thin you felt sorry for him when he wore a short-sleeved shirt. His wrists looked like they might break any minute. He was a Puerto Rican with short, curly hair, a mousy face, and a thin moustache I thought made him look like a fag.

"Yo, bro', lend me five-hun'red dollars!"

"Say what?"

"Man, I need five-hun'red dollars. I swear I'll pay you back in two weeks. Just give me two weeks, and I'll pay you back. Come on, Tito."

Pepito hardly ever called me by my name. It was usually "Bro" or "Man." So when he called me Tito, I knew something wasn't right.

"Why you need five-hundred dollars for?"

"Yo, Tito, just help me out, all right? I'll pay you back."

Pepito was usually a milk-and-coffee-brown color. But he looked white to me.

"Pepo, I ain't got that kinda money on me. What you want it for?"

"If I tell you, you lend it to me?" he asked, looking desperate.

"Yeah, okay," I said, but I really didn't want to. Pepito was my best friend, but five-hundred dollars was quite a bit of money to give away. When you lend a friend money, you never see a cent of it again.

Pepito said, "I lost some money in a bet, and when it was time to pay, I didn't have it. They told me they was going to kill me if I didn't pay them by tonight. That's why I need it, Tito. If I don't pay, they'll kill me!"

"Who's they, man?"

"These guys."

"Who?"

Pepito didn't answer right away. He was thinking.

"Chimp and his boys. You don't know them, but they run numbers down in Harlem. I laid the bet *mano limpia.* Somebody tipped me off on the number. But that number didn't come up."

"Why'd you bet so much?"

"I was tipped off, man. I thought I had them by the balls. Now they got me by the balls."

"All right," I said. "I don't got any money here. I gotta go to the bank."

"So go get it."

"Not now. You said you got to pay them by tonight, right? Let me cook some breakfast first."

"You bring it to me?"

"Sure, just let me eat first."

"All right, Tito, I'll be home. Just come by as soon as you eat."

Pepito opened the door and left. I locked it and went to fry my eggs. Pepito had been running around doing crazy things since we were kids. He used to like to go down to the railroad tracks by the Henry Hudson Parkway and throw rocks at the bums who lived in that desolate area. I used to go with him, just for the fun of it, but I stopped throwing rocks when I saw Pepito hit a bum square in the face. The bum lived in a shack built into a grassy rise filled with trash, tires and discarded car parts. We called him names until he came out, and then Pepito hit him with a big rock and his face split open like a watermelon.

As soon as I was done eating, I went over to my girl-friend's place near Broadway, just past Trinity Cemetery. I didn't live too far from her. My *Papi* and *Mami* came from Cuba in the sixties and settled in the Heights. Decent people existed back then, but now all you saw was *dominicanos* and *puertorriqueños,* and to the east in Harlem, the blacks.

My bank was downtown, and there were no cash machines in my neighborhood. So I decided to bum the money off of her until Monday. Her name was Mircea. She was Puerto Rican, petite, with nice olive skin, blonde-dyed hair, widely spaced black eyes, and a smile that could drive you crazy. Her mother, Mrs. Corteza, opened the door for me. She was proud of me because I could pass for white if I really tried. I was actually Mircea's color, due mostly to the sun, but I looked like a Spaniard. It was a good thing for a dark-skin to catch a light-skin, like Mircea did me. My mother knew this Dominican who was as black as any black. One of his sons went to Germany with the Army and married a blonde white girl over

Project Death: A Tito Rico Mystery

there. My mother asked him if he would have preferred his son to marry a black woman, and he told her, "Black? Why? We've got enough black in the family."

Mrs. Corteza didn't speak any English, but I liked talking in Spanish when I was at Mircea's place. But when I was alone with Mircea, we spoke English, or a mixture of the two.

"How are you, Tito, come in please, did you eat, I do not think you ate, let me boil you some plantains and fry you some eggs, how about it, I know you are hungry," Mrs. Corteza said to me in one Spanish breath as I stepped in.

"No, thank you, Mrs. Corteza."

"Mircea!" she called, and followed me down the hall into the living room, where Mircea's twenty-year old brother José was watching a video.

"Yo, Tito," he greeted me without taking his eyes off the television. It was a Schwarzenegger movie. I could hear the noise of the violence from the end of the hall. José was still trying to finish high school. He had been going off and on for the past six years. He worked at this *bodega* down on 139th.

Mircea came out of her room, came to me, and kissed me. She was wearing a tan halter-top and a pair of tight-fitting blue jeans with expert rips across the thighs.

"Hi, baby," she said. "I thought you weren't coming to see me today."

"Mircea, I got to talk to you. Can we go in your room?"

I remembered Mrs. Corteza was still behind me. I looked back at her and smiled. "We're just going to talk, Mrs. Corteza."

Mircea's mother was a devout Catholic who didn't allow any foolishness in her house. I could be alone anywhere with Mircea except in her own room. But I understood that and didn't mind.

Mircea took me by the hand and we went into her room. She was twenty-six but still decorated her room like a little girl. The dolls she so prized when she was a kid were neatly dressed and sitting or standing on shelves and furniture. Her dresser was a storefront of perfume bottles and talc boxes. The comforter on her bed was pink and had azure ruffles along the edge.

I sat on the bed, and Mircea sat on me. Since I was there, I kissed her for a while.

"Baby," I said, "I need you to lend me five-hundred dollars."

"What?"

"It's not for me. It's for Pepito. He got in a little trouble. I got the money in the bank and will pay you back on Monday. I promise."

"Ha! Pepito is always in trouble," she said as she stood up and went to a drawer of her dresser and took out a cigar box. She came back to sit next to me. "Why you keep on helping him? He's never going to change."

"He's my friend."

"Friend? What's he ever done for you, Tito?"

"A lot. We're buddies. We grew up together in the 'hood. You know?"

"I don't know," she said as she counted off five hundred dollars into my palm from a wad that contained much more.

"How much you got there?" I asked.

"None o' your business," she said playfully.

"What you saving up for?"

"For when we get married."

She was always bringing up marriage. Not intrusively, but when the conversation gave an opportunity. The last thing I wanted to do was get married. I liked us just the way we were.

"Well, keep on saving," I said as I stood up. She shook her head.

"You're going to go?"

"I got to get this money to Pepito."

"Stay a little while. Let's go out."

"I got to work on my car today. It's been sitting outside my building for two weeks."

"Do it tomorrow."

"No."

"So you came here just to get the money?"

"Yeah."

She sucked her teeth loudly and stood up. But she smiled as she reached up to put her arms around my neck. I kissed her and didn't want to leave. But I had to leave when Mrs. Corteza began knocking on the door.

"I don't hear talking!" she shouted through the door.

Mircea wiped the beige lipstick around my mouth with her fingers. She glanced in her mirror before opening the door.

"I was just leaving," I said.

Mrs. Corteza's face softened to a concerned frown.

"No, stay a little while!"

"Thanks, Mrs. Corteza, but I got to go work on my car."

I turned to Mircea and winked at her. I kissed her mother on the cheek and said good-bye to José. I heard him say "Yo" as I left the apartment.

Pepito's building faced LaSalle Street, and two walking paths cut through a playground to the street. There were two ambulances parked on the street and three police cars. A crowd of people was standing around the entrance to the building and sitting on nearby benches. They were very quiet. Cops were standing around, their radios scratching away. They weren't letting anyone in or out of the building. I watched, waiting to see what happened. Somebody came to stand next to me and asked me what was going on. When I said I had no idea, an old woman, standing in front of me, turned around.

"They kilt somebody up there!"

"Who?" I asked.

"Don't know that. But they kilt somebody."

While I waited, another police car ripped down the street with its siren screaming. The cops who got out of that car talked with some of the cops who were standing around and then went into the building. Ten minutes later paramedics came out of the building pushing a cart with somebody under a white sheet. There was a large red stain on the sheet where the head would be. The cops pushed some people aside to make way for the paramedics. I was intent on looking at the body on the cart when a woman ran out of the building screaming. When I saw who it was, my heart stopped, and for a second I thought I was next to drop dead. It was Maritza, Pepito's eighteen-year-old sister. She was thin like her brother, and her mousy face stuck out because she wore her hair in a tight ponytail. Two cops grabbed her and pulled her back inside. With my heart still in my throat, I looked up at the paramedics who were halfway to the ambulances. Then I ran after them. A cop behind them turned around and stuck his

Project Death: A Tito Rico Mystery

hand out, but I was running so fast that I nearly knocked him over. The other cops managed to pin my arms behind me, but not before I pulled away the sheet from the body. Underneath was Pepito, as white as the sheet that covered him, with a gash from one ear to the other. A mess of gauze was stuck into the wound, and there was blood under his head and around his neck. The sight was so horrible that it was good the cops pulled me back.

"What the fuck you doing?" one of them yelled in my ear.

"He's my friend!" I cried

"You know 'im?" the other cop yelled.

"He's my friend!" I cried again.

That was enough for them. They relaxed their grip on me when I calmed down. They pulled me over and put me in a squad car. A few minutes later, I was sitting in the 27th Precinct.

CHAPTER TWO

The 27th was on 127th Street, a street that was probably the safest in all of Harlem. They had me wait about a half-hour in a room full of sweaty, nervous-looking people. I'm sure I looked as bad as they did. I couldn't get Pepito out of my mind. There were screams in my head, my own and Maritza's. They were so loud I thought the other people could hear them. But they must have been preoccupied with their own screams.

A middle-aged white man with a red, spongy face, thin brown hair, a black suit, and fifties-looking glasses stood at the door with a file in his hand and called my name. He nodded at me and I followed him to a room full of cubicles. His was in a corner, under a window frosted over and sealed shut.

"Have a seat, Mr. Rico," he said after roughly clearing his throat. I sat on a folding chair next to his desk.

"How long have you known the victim?" he asked.

"Since I was seven," I said, "about twenty-four years."

"I'm Detective Krieger, by the way," he said, and then cleared his throat again. That gave me the chance to ask him the question I most dreaded.

Project Death: A Tito Rico Mystery

"He's really dead?"

"Yes, he's dead."

I knew he was. The white sheet wouldn't have been over his face if he wasn't. And that cut, nobody could have survived that. There's no doctor alive who could stop the blood on a cut like that.

Detective Krieger drained the coffee from a cup on his desk. Then he took out a pen and asked me about myself, where I lived, were I worked, what I was doing near the projects. He was surprised when I told him I worked as a cleaner for the Transit Authority. His nephew was recently hired as a Transit Cop.

"What time did Mr. Espinoza come to see you this morning?"

"It must've been around nine."

"Did you notice any bruises on him?"

"No, he was just nervous. And pale."

"This guy he mentioned to you, Chimp, you know him?"

"No."

"So you don't know if that's his real name or what?"

"I don't know, but they probably just call him that."

"Did Mr. Espinoza tell you where Chimp was or where he was going to deliver the money?"

"Just that Chimp was in Harlem. He didn't say where."

A cop passed by and threw a file on Detective Krieger's desk. Krieger opened it and looked through the papers.

"Mmm. . ."

I glanced over.

"You have a juvenile record, Mr. Rico. In 1975, arrested for destruction of private property; 1977, cited for driving without a license. Same year, arrested for driving without a license and driving intoxicated. In 1978, cited for disorderly conduct. And there's more."

I shrugged my shoulders. "That was when I was a kid. Me and Pepito used to do crazy things."

"How crazy?"

"Well, it never got worse than that. We never killed nobody."

Detective Krieger closed my file. "You ever play the numbers?" he asked.

"Well, yeah, sometimes."

"You ever go into Harlem to play the numbers?"

"Nah, for what? They got that in the Heights."

"Did Mr. Espinoza have any enemies?"

I thought a second. Sure he did, so did I. But they were the kind of enemies that would set fire to your car or throw rocks through your living room window. But as far as I knew, Pepito didn't have any enemies that would murder him. And neither did I.

"No," I said.

"Well," Detective Krieger said, "thank you for your cooperation."

He verified my address. "We'll be in contact with you if we have any more questions."

He sat back in his chair and waited for me to get up. But I didn't.

"You're going to look for this guy?"

"What guy?"

"The guy who killed Pepito."

"We'll investigate the matter."

"You got to catch him."

"We'll do all we can."

Project Death: A Tito Rico Mystery

I started to get angry because Pepito was dead and here we were talking very civilly about "an investigation." I could tell this guy didn't give a damn about what happened. He was just doing his job, waiting for the five-o'clock whistle. A dead spic or nigger in the projects was all in a day's business.

"Thanks," I said, getting up fast and almost taking the metal chair with me. As I left the room I could feel him looking at me.

⋙ ⋙ ⋙

I walked from the precinct back to the projects. Everything was back to normal. Old people were sitting on the benches by the playground in front, and big kids were swinging on small swings. There wasn't a cop anywhere. I went into the building and waited a long time for the elevator. When it finally came down, a large group of people got off.

Pepito's mother, Catalina Espinoza, and his two sisters lived on the eighteenth floor. There were a lot of people on the floor, standing in and around the door of the apartment. I made my way through the crowd until Mrs. Espinoza, standing at the door in a blue cotton nightgown, saw me. Her eyes were red and swollen, and her already old face looked even older. She had a blue handkerchief in her hand. When she saw me, she wailed and held her arms out for me. People made way for me as I approached and hugged her. All she was doing was wailing my name and Pepito's name. The people around the door were talking and shaking their heads.

Mrs. Espinoza was a short, fat woman who liked to cook. You never saw her out of her nightgown or out of the kitchen. She was always very happy and smiling, and it broke my heart to see her like this. She pulled me into the apartment and to a couch. There were other people in the house sitting on every available seat. I recognized one old lady who lived next door. She was sitting in an easy chair with her cane between her legs. Everybody was talking, Spanish and English flying back and forth. Mrs. Espinoza sat next to me and I just didn't know what to say.

"They kill Pepito!" she sobbed.

"I know, I know."

"Who kill my son? Why they kill my son?"

"Where did it happen?"

"They find him in the stairs. *¡Ay, Dios!*"

"What floor?"

"Tenth floor."

"Where are Maritza and Tina?"

"I don't know. They go. They no want to be here."

Mrs. Espinoza began to cry in her handkerchief. Someone brought her a glass of water. More and more people seemed to be crowding around the door, trying to take a look in. I glanced around and saw this black guy picking up a crystal polyhedron with a gold coin suspended in the center from a bookshelf. He thought nobody was looking and tried to pocket it. I got up fast and cursed him. He got scared, dropped it on the floor, and pushed his way out. I then began to throw everybody out. I must have been rude because some of the people cursed at me. But I threw everybody out except the old neighbor lady and another old lady who was Mrs. Espinoza's friend. I walked Pepito's mother to her room and then got myself a glass of water to alleviate my dry throat. When they were all gone and it was quiet, I stepped out and walked down a nar-

Project Death: A Tito Rico Mystery

row, smelly, graffiti-covered stairwell to the tenth landing. An old black porter in gray overalls was on his knees, his sleeves rolled up past his elbows, scrubbing the floor by the door with a soapy sponge. When he saw me, he dipped the sponge in a bucket and squeezed it so that most of the water splashed out.

"Somethin' wrong with d'elevators?" he asked me.

"Nah, they're all right. Is this where it happened?"

He reached out an arm and pulled the metal door toward him. "That's where d'blood start."

He pointed out a blotch on the hard and shiny floor at the base of the door.

"Spill'd out here."

There was no blood left on the outside of the door, which was directly in front of the door to apartment 10G. There was only a very clean spot where the old man had scrubbed. He let the door close.

"You see anything?" I asked.

"No, I was down in d'basement when't happen'd. You know 'im?"

"Yeah."

"Damn shame, all's I could say."

He went back to scrubbing. I could see a layer of dried blood on the outside of his left leg. He saw it too and began scrubbing that. I opened the door and stepped into the hallway. One end was dark because the light on the ceiling was broken. It was quiet and there was nothing unusual. I looked at the walls for blood, but I didn't see any, although I might have missed some among the graffiti.

I took the elevator back down and walked up Lasalle Street to Broadway. In front of a playground near the corner was a police car. There were three cops inside and one leaning in talking through the passenger window. I looked at them as I passed them. They stopped talking and looked back at me. The driver and the cop in the back were white. The one in the passenger seat and the one outside were black. They looked at me until I arrived at the corner, and were still looking at me as I turned and walked to the train.

When I got home, I cried a little when I realized that Pepito was dead. It never hits you right away. I remember when my father died, when I was twelve. I didn't cry for three weeks. Then all of a sudden, I just started crying while I was in church with my mother. That Sunday I went, and started crying while I was sitting down listening to the priest giving a prayer. Everybody turned around to look, but I didn't care. My mother pulled my head to her, held me there a while, and then led me out. I thought I wasn't going to stop crying.

CHAPTER THREE

That night I walked to a bar called Nig's on St. Nicholas Avenue. It was my usual hangout when I didn't have much to do. There was just a door and a smoky window with a neon beer sign, so smoky that you couldn't see in at all. It was always dark inside, too. There was a bar against the wall across from the entrance, a pool table at the back which nobody used except to rest glasses and bottles on, and half a dozen round tables. There was always an equal mix of blacks and Hispanics. The owner was Mike Crowe, a thin black man who spent most of his time at his other bar on 148th and Lenox Avenue. But when he was at Nig's, he would sit in a corner playing cards or dominoes with his friends. I didn't know him that well, but he nodded at me when he saw me, just like he did to all his regular customers.

It always took a minute for my eyes to get accustomed to the dim light in Nig's. As soon as I was acclimated, I sat at the bar and asked Martin, the bartender, for a beer. He was a large, powerfully built man from Barbados who spoke with a very pronounced accent. I couldn't understand him half the time and so nodded whenever he spoke to me. Despite his size and strength, he was an amazingly gentle man who was always smiling. There was never any trouble at Nig's anyway.

"Yah look kind'a down, Rico," he said to me as he popped off the lid to my Heineken.

He didn't know Pepito, so I didn't want to get into what happened.

"Just tired," I said.

"Well, naow, this will cheer y'up."

He gave me the bottle and I downed half of it.

"Look o'er there, naow," Martin said, pointing into the darkness of the other side of the room. "Tell me yah don't remember that character."

I peered to where he pointed and saw a black man sitting alone at a table. He had both elbows on the table and seemed as if he was trying to support his torso from falling over. Rhythmically he sagged and pushed himself up. I couldn't be sure, but I got the impression it was my old friend, Alonzo Casimire Brown.

"That ain't...," I was about to say.

"Tha's him. Got out o' jail three days 'go."

I took my bottle and stood in front of Alonzo. He was about my height, five-feet eleven, but twice as wide as me. He was one solid human being, with constantly perspiring skin the color of rotting bananas. His face and nose were broad, and his eyes cunning because of his usual, menacing smile. Seven years ago he caught a man in bed with his girl and killed him. Since then he was at a pen in Arizona. Apart from getting sturdier, he had not changed. He was sitting drunk, dressed in a white shirt, gray acrylic pants, and a matching jacket.

Project Death: A Tito Rico Mystery

There was a bottle of French brandy in his hand, almost empty, and two glasses between his arms. When he noticed me, he looked up slowly without a smile.

"What the fuck you want?"

I got scared for a moment. Alonzo was one man you didn't mess with. We had been friends since grade school, running around doing wild things. It was him, me, Pepito, and three other guys who always hanged together. But Alonzo was the toughest. And when he got his first gun at age twelve, he was the man.

"Alonzo, it's me, Tito," I said fast. "Tito Rico."

He looked at me a moment longer and then smiled. I felt relieved.

"M-a-a-a-a-n," he said, pushing himself up.

"Just got out, huh?" I asked.

Alonzo took one step forward and fell onto me in an embrace. I could feel something long and hard in his jacket pocket.

"Wassup, man?" he said.

I embraced him to steady him, and brought him back down to his seat.

"Where you been, man?" he asked.

"Where you been?"

"You know where I been. Out o' that shit, though."

"You were there a long time."

"Too long. Them muthafuckas put me 'way too long. They wuz goin'a make it fifteen. But I was good's an angel. You know, don't ever kill nobody over a ho', all right? Ho's ain't worth it. But I done right, I done right. I try t 'tell the judge what I felt when I saw that ho' with that sonofabitch. That white muthafucka, what he do if he got his fat ass off that bench, went home, an' found me fuckin' his bitch? He'd grab wutever the fuck he got and shoot the black shit outta me. That shit ain't right, y'know?"

Alonzo only swore a lot when he was drunk, so I could tell he was really drunk. He had always carried a gun since he was twelve and was quick to use it whenever something bothered him. He had come home early from work one night to find this girl he was staying with in bed with another guy. Alonzo told me that what bothered him was that they were doing it in the open, and not under the sheets. If they had been covered up, he told me would only have beaten up the guy. But when he saw their sweaty bodies, and the shame of it, he could do nothing less that take out his gun and fire.

"Where you staying, Alonzo?"

"With a lady o' mine. How you been?"

I was unsure whether to mention Pepito. We were all close when we were young. In Alonzo's state, I was afraid of a bad reaction.

"You hear about Pepito?"

"Pepito? Yea, how's Pepito?"

"He got murdered."

Alonzo looked at me strangely. His smile contracted slowly.

"Wassat?"

"He got killed today. Somebody cut his neck."

"Nah, nah."

"Yeah."

"You buggin' me? Who'd wanna kill Pepito?"

"I ain't lying. I went over to see him at the projects down on 125th, and I saw him being carried out under a sheet. The cops took me in for questioning."

Project Death: A Tito Rico Mystery

Alonzo stared down at the brandy bottle and shook his head.

"Oh, man. Who did't?"

"Nobody knows. He came over to my place this morning to borrow some money. He said he owed it to this bookie named Chimp, and that Chimp was going to kill him if he didn't pay him by tonight. When I went over to take him the money, he was dead."

"Chimp?"

"Yeah. You know him?"

"Never heard'a him. Where he work?"

"Pepito told me in Harlem."

"Shit, man. Pepito was my friend."

"Yeah, I know."

"I got out just in time."

"For what?"

"We got to find this muthafucka."

"Chimp?"

"We got to find him an' kill him."

"What you talking about?"

"Me an' you, Tito. We find him an' kill him. You know the po-lice ain't gonna do shit. What you say?"

"We just can't go and find him and kill him."

"Why not?" Alonzo said, patting his jacket pocket. "I done it before."

I thought of when I pulled back Pepito's sheet and saw the horrible cut and all the blood. They didn't have to kill him that way.

"At least we can try to find him."

"You do what you want. I find 'im, I'll cap 'im."

"You think we can do it?"

"Whoever kill Pepito is dead."

He stuck out his hand. I should have thought about it some more, but I grabbed his hand and we shook the way we used to do it when we were young. I did it on the impulse, because I was mad and wanted revenge. But then I started to regret what I was doing. I knew it could only be more trouble because once you shake like that, your committed to whatever you're going to do.

CHAPTER FOUR

I couldn't sleep much of the night. Pepito was on my mind. At one point, I was dreaming about him. The way I grew up, when dead people come into your dreams, it means their ghost was really there in the room with you. That's why my mother would cross my slippers and put a glass of water in a corner of my room when I was a kid. The cross would keep the ghosts away, and if that didn't work, the water would suck them in if they tried to take a drink. And ghosts were always thirsty, especially if they died thirsty. I've heard it said that most people get thirsty right before they die. But I didn't believe much of that anymore. My mother grew up in the country in Cuba, where superstitions from Catholicism and African religions were the norm. When the slaves were brought over to the island, they were forced to convert to Catholicism by the Spaniards. But they still kept their old animistic beliefs. The mixture was called *santería*. Every African god had a counterpart as a Catholic saint.

So I don't know if Pepito's ghost came to me as I slept. If he did, he didn't come looking scary. I was dreaming that me and him were hanging out in front of the building drinking fortys. Alonzo was with us, too, and the three other members of our posse: Hector, Indio, and Little Louie. Hector got his girlfriend pregnant four years ago, got married, and moved up to the Bronx. Indio went into the Marines, and we lost track of him. And the last time I heard from Little Louie, he was living in Brooklyn. But in those days, we were all free and happy. We did whatever we wanted whenever we wanted. It was a nice existence.

I finally fell into a deep sleep around five in the morning. Around eleven, a loud knock on my door woke me up. It was Alonzo. I had thought that he said what he said at the bar because he was drunk, and that once sober he would have forgotten all about our vendetta. But he was sober now, and as determined as ever.

"Wassup, man?" he said, came in, and threw himself on the couch.

"What's up, Alonzo?"

"You ready?"

"For what?"

"We're gonna find Chimp."

Alonzo took out a Glock 9mm from under his shirt and put it on the couch next to him.

"What if we get caught?"

"Fuck that. We ain't getting caught."

"Where we start?"

"Boot town, man."

"What we gonna do, go around asking for him?"

Project Death: A Tito Rico Mystery

"He runs numbers, right? People'll know. You got food?"

I pointed him to the kitchen. He ate while I showered and dressed. I didn't have a gun, but I had a three-inch knife that I carried around under my shirt when I was working. I worked the number 4 train and stations from Flatbush to Woodlawn in the Bronx, the four-to-midnight shift one week and the regular the next. There have been only two attempts to mug me since I started working. The first time, the two guys got away with my wallet. The second, I took out my knife and stabbed the mugger in the arm. I don't know why anybody would want to mug a train sweeper.

We took the train down to 125th and then walked east. 125th is crazy on Sunday mornings. The streets are filled with people and vendors, selling everything from African *kente* cloth to handbags to jewelry to video tapes and cassettes. Before a movie is released on video, you can get a hot copy on 125th Street. Sometimes movies aren't even out yet in the theaters, and you can buy a copy of it on tape. I don't know who said that there aren't a lot of blacks in the movies. All I know is that they *got* the movies.

We stopped at a few vendors and started some chitchat, which led to talk about the numbers. Most of them are Africans or from the islands and don't really know what's going on. They live in the Bronx and come down to sell their wares, sometimes homemade, like paintings and clothes. But there was one guy, a savage-looking black man in army fatigues, who was taking photographs of people in front of colorful graffiti murals for three dollars. Tourists could have a picture taken and say they visited Harlem, I guessed. He was sitting on a chair next to a radio playing Ice-T.

"We're looking for a brother they call Chimp," Alonzo said to him. "We heard he's got good stakes."

The man looked at us, reached down, and turned up the radio.

"We ain't Five-O, man," Alonzo said, taking out a ten-dollar bill. The man held out his palm until Alonzo put a bill there.

"He's gonna run 'em this afternoon," the man said. "Next to the bakery by Fifth."

Alonzo looked at me, nodded, and we continued to walk.

"I'm sure he's got men there," I said.

"You know he does."

"We just can't go in there."

"We're gonna scope the place first. If we have to come back, we will."

We crossed Lenox and started looking for a bakery. The only one between Lenox and Fifth was across the street from where we were. Next to it was a small toy shop with a filthy sign and filthy windows. On display were a few sorry-looking ten-year-old toys covered with dust. It was all a front. We went in and there was a room full of men, sitting and standing, smoking and with beer bottles in their hands. There was a line in front of a doorway covered with a shower curtain. We stood on line, Alonzo in front of me. The line moved fast, as men came in and out, and in a minute or two we were in a little room facing a man sitting behind a desk. He was dressed in a brown suit and his collar was open at the neck. He looked about fifty and completely bald, with a head like a gourd and a large jaw. His lower lip stuck out farther than the top and there was a large crumb stuck on it. There was an ashtray by his arm with a dozen spent cigarettes. As soon as we came in, he put a fresh one in his mouth and lit it.

"Six or eight?" he asked without looking up at us. He was ready to write something down.

"You Chimp?" Alonzo said.

The man looked up slowly. He took the cigarette out of his mouth with a hand covered with gold rings. It seemed time froze for a long time.

"Rocky!" he yelled, and shot to his feet. I heard the curtain ruffle behind me and turned to see two big men come in. I looked back and saw that Alonzo had the tip of his gun touching Chimp's forehead.

"You killed my friend, muthafucka," Alonzo said quietly. Chimp's eyes turned from his gun to the two men who came in. One of them asked Alonzo what the hell he was doing.

"Daddy here killed a friend of mine," Alonzo said. "And if you niggers don't get out, I'm'a kill you, too."

"I did'n kill nobody, man!" Chimp said, sliding back down to his seat without his forehead losing contact with Alonzo's gun. His voice was loud, but he was still as a rock.

"Pepito, he owed you some money," I said, stepping aside so my back wasn't to the two men. "He was going to pay you, but you killed him."

"Listen, man," Chimp said. "I don't know what you talking about. I've never seen you in my life and I didn' kill nobody."

"That's it," Alonzo said to me, "I'm'a kill this muthafucka."

Everybody in the room was very still for a moment. I was afraid that Alonzo would pull the trigger before I had a chance to say something. For some reason, I had the feeling that

Chimp was right, that he didn't kill Pepito. He probably did-n't even know who Pepito was.

"A, let's go," I said.

"What?"

"He didn't do it. Let's go."

"Damn right, I didn't do it," Chimp muttered. "Don't know what you talking about."

Alonzo gave me a helpless look and then pointed the gun at the two men. They stepped aside so we could pass. In the other room, most of the men were standing around the door, curious about what was happening. As soon as they saw the gun, they stepped aside. But we got out with no problem.

We walked out looking behind us just in case Chimp sent one of his men after us. When we were a block away, we relaxed.

"What you mean he didn't kill Pepito?" Alonzo asked me. "Didn't Pepito say it was him?"

"He did, but I think he was lying. Didn't you see Chimp when you had that gun against his head? He didn't even move. He didn't seem afraid because he knew he was inno-cent. If he had killed Pepito, he would've acted differently."

"You crazy, Tito. We had him."

"Plus, when I asked Pepito what was wrong, it was like he was making stuff up. It wasn't Chimp."

"But how you know?"

"I just know, A. Why would Pepito be playing down here? You know how he hated niggers except you. Why not with the usual guys up in the Heights?"

"So who did it?"

Project Death: A Tito Rico Mystery

I looked down the busy street, teeming with colorful people. It was a different world up here, with different rules. I
didn't know who killed Pepito, or why. And I admitted it.

CHAPTER FIVE

Alonzo was staying with this woman named Roxanne and her little daughter in her small apartment on the corner of 132nd and Seventh. Roxanne was slim and about a foot shorter than me. She was beautiful, the way working-class black women are beautiful. They don't have much, but what they got they use or wear with great dignity. Alonzo told me she was a clerk for one of the city departments downtown, the Department of the Aging, or something similar. Her hair was short and pressed back in shiny waves. Her skin color was a dark amber, and her face was wide. She looked like she had some Oriental blood in her because her eyes were slightly slanting.

"Hey, baby," Alonzo said, and kissed Roxanne when we came in. She had been busy feeding her daughter, a fidgety three-year old named Moniqua, on the living room floor. "This's my buddy Tito. We go back."

"Hi." Roxanne held out her hand and I took it. She regarded me a moment and then went back to her daughter.

"I boiled some greens, if you want 'em," she said.

Project Death: A Tito Rico Mystery

Alonzo and I sat at the table in the kitchen and talked in hushed tones so that Roxanne wouldn't hear. But I knew that she was trying to listen because she would keep glancing at the clock on the wall behind us.

"I need to find out more, talk to some people, gather more information," I said.

"I'll be here. You let me know what's up."

"You ain't working?"

"Nah. Roxanne's taking care of me. I'm free all day."

"All right, I'll get back to you as soon as I find out something."

"Listen, Tito, I've known you since we were kids. I know you've never killed a man. That's why I'm here, all right? You leave all the dirty work to me. Just find out who did it, and I'll take care of the rest."

⟨✦⟩ ⟨✦⟩ ⟨✦⟩

I had to be at work at four that afternoon because that week I was on the late shift. On Wednesday, I took off to go to Pepito's funeral. The undertaker did a good job sewing Pepito up. He had one of those Italian shirts on under his suit with a high collar to cover the wound. I stood over him a long time at the funeral home, just looking at him. I wanted to lay a hand on his folded hands, but I was afraid. I had only done that once before, after my father died when I was twelve. At his wake, I was expecting him to jump up out of the coffin. When I touched his cold, hard hands, I thought he was going to grab my arm. So I didn't touch Pepito. I didn't want to feel his coldness.

On Saturday I worked for most of the day on my Subaru.
I had a feeling I was going to need it. In the afternoon I went
over to the projects again to see Pepito's mother and his sisters. Mrs. Espinoza was still in mourning and would be so for
a few months. She had all the pictures she had of Pepito out in
the living room. There was Pepito when he was just a kid,
when he was running around with me, and recent pictures. In
one picture, our posse was hanging out on the steps of a building. I was sitting between Pepito and Hector. Alonzo, Indio,
and Little Louie were standing behind us making gestures
behind our back. None of us were older than sixteen.

Tina, Pepito's fifteen-year-old sister, was out with her
friends. But Maritza was home and we went to the playground. We sat side by side on swings. Maritza was in her last
year of high school and unsure of what to do next. She had a
boyfriend who wanted her to live with him, but Mrs. Espinoza
was against this. She was pretty, with long dark hair pulled
tight against her head, red lipstick, and a set of perfect, white,
baby teeth.

"You okay?" I asked.

"Nah, Tito."

"How's Tina taking it?"

"She cries every night. None of us can believe it yet, you
know what I'm saying?"

"Yeah, yeah."

We sat there a long time and rocked gently.

"Your brother ever talk to you about his business?"

"Not really."

"He never told you where he was going or what he was
doing?"

"Sometimes."

"In the past few weeks, did he have people over at the apartment?"

"Sometimes."

"Who?"

"His friend Noel."

"Who's he?"

"A guy he was hanging out with. He lives in another building."

"Anybody else?"

"On Friday night, he had this argument with this guy. He's the president of the Tenants' Association."

"Friday before he died?"

"Yeah."

"In the house?"

"No, outside, out here."

Maritza pointed at the entrance of her building. There were three steel doors, beaten up and without handles, in between windows covered with metal grates.

"What happened?"

"I don't know. I was coming down, ready to go out, when I saw Pepito arguing with Mr. Braxton. It looked like Mr. Braxton wanted to hit him."

"Did Pepito tell you about it after?"

"No."

"Where does this guy live?"

"Fourteen or fifteen, I think."

A police car was cruising up the street. The two cops were two of the guys I had seen the day Pepito was murdered. The driver was the same white guy for sure, and the other one was one of the black cops. They didn't see me, but I looked at their faces. They were looking into the complex, squinting their eyes. The white cop had brown hair and moustache. The black guy was dark-skinned, with a big mouth, and wore glasses. I was watching them pass when I heard Maritza sob. She didn't want me to see her cry, so she turned her head away.

"It's all right," I said, and reached out my hand to touch her back. She was about to really cry.

"I gotta go, okay?" she said, and got off the swing. I stood up.

"I'll walk you back."

I walked Maritza inside the building and waited for the elevator with her. When it came, she kissed me on my cheek and got on. I was about to go out when a man called to me in a guttural voice.

"Yo, help me out!"

A crack head was standing by the mailboxes. He was thin and stooped over, unshaven, and had that blank stare that meant he was due for another fix.

"Yo, brother, help me out!"

"What you want?" I asked.

The crack head was trying to stick his key in his mailbox, but his hand was shaking so bad that he kept missing the lock. I went over, took the key, opened the small mailbox and handed him his letters, one a Con Ed bill and the other a Publisher's Clearing House sweepstakes letter.

"Yeah, yeah, thanks," he said, and turned away, his mailbox still open. I shook my head and snapped it shut. As I did so I noticed how dirty my hands were from working on the car that morning.

Project Death: A Tito Rico Mystery

⬥⬥⬥

"Open up, Police!" was what I heard at about two Sunday morning. I got up from bed as fast as I could because I didn't want my door busted in, which was what was going to happen if I didn't open up. There were five cops, two white and three black, with their guns drawn.

"What's going on?" I managed to say before they all rushed in and locked handcuffs on me.

"Shut the fuck up! You're under arrest!" one of them said. So I shut up and ducked my head as I was led out of the building and into a waiting squad car. I didn't say a word until I was back at the 27th.

⬥⬥⬥

I was put in a cell with ten other guys for about an hour. I had managed to grab a jacket before I was cuffed, but other than that, all I had on was my sleeping clothes: sweat pants and a t-shirt. Two cops took me in an elevator to another floor and to a brightly lit room with a small table in the middle, surrounded by shade-covered windows. A white man in a taupe poplin suit was sitting at one end, a woman next to him. He looked about thirty-five, maybe forty, with short, shellacked hair, a narrow, pointy face and round gold-framed glasses. The woman was black and dumpy, with badly straightened hair and thick Coke-bottle glasses.

"Have a seat, Mr. Rico," the man said, pointing to the chair next to him and across from the woman.

When I sat down, he asked me, "Do you understand what I'm saying?"

I looked at him strange, nodded my head, and said, "Yeah, I do."

"He understands English," the man said to the woman. "We won't be needing you."

The woman, who I guessed was an interpreter, left the room with the two cops. At that moment, Detective Krieger came in. His hair was messy and he wore no tie. He looked like he had just left his bed.

"Detective," the man said.

Krieger looked at me and sat where the woman had been.

"You've met Detective Krieger," the man said. "I'm Detective Harrell."

"Rico," Krieger said to me. "Do you know why you're here?"

"That's just what I was about to ask."

"Do you know a man by the name of Wayne Edgar Jones?"

"Never heard of him."

"You sure?" Harrell asked.

"Yeah, I am."

"Where we're you last night around eleven?"

"At home, in my bed."

"Did you visit 23 Lasalle Street anytime up to eleven last night?"

I had no idea what they were getting at, but they wanted to nail me for something. So I decided to be completely honest.

"Yesterday afternoon, I was there."

"What time?" Krieger asked.

"Around three or four."

"What were you doing there?"

"I went to see Pepito's mother."

"When did you leave the building?"

"Around five, I think."

"Where did you go after that?"

"Home."

"Did you return to the building at any time after that?"

"No, I went home."

Krieger folded his hands on the table.

"There was another murder, Rico. Last night. One Wayne Edgar Jones was found shot to death in the basement of 23 Lasalle Street."

Harrell reached down beside him, opened a briefcase, and took out a manila envelope. From that he took out two large photographs and lay them on the table.

"Recognize this man?"

I looked at the pictures. A black man was lying on the ground. In his dead state he didn't look much like the crack head I helped with his mailbox, but I knew it was him.

"Yeah, I've seen him."

"Where?" Harrell pressed.

"At the building. I saw him yesterday before I left. He was trying to open his mailbox, and I helped him out."

"You helped him open his mailbox?" Krieger asked.

"Yeah. Guy was shaking so bad he couldn't fit the key in the lock."

"There were clear fingerprints on two letters found in his apartment," Harrell said. "They matched yours."

"I told you," I said excitedly. "I told you straight out that I got his mail out for him."

I looked at Krieger. "I told you. I ain't hiding anything. I got his letters out, a bill from Con Ed and one of those magazine sweepstakes letters. I gave them to him and that's the last I saw the man."

"Do you have anyone who can corroborate this?" Harrell asked.

"What? That I gave him the letters and that was that? I don't know. But you can ask Mrs. Espinoza and Maritza, and they'll tell you I was there. I was talking with Maritza out in the park, then I walked her to the elevator. That was it. Then I went home."

"Right now, you are our main suspect."

"I didn't do it, man!"

"Don't get excited, Rico," Krieger said.

"Don't get excited? I'm telling you, I didn't do it. You saying I killed Pepito, too, my best friend?"

"You happened to be at the projects when your friend was found, too," Harrell said.

"Detective Krieger knows why I was there. He knows the whole story. Something's up here, and you guys better get out there and find out who's doing the killings. You're wasting your time with me."

Harrell began to clean his glasses on his tie. He was thin, but tall, with an athletic build.

"I'm tired, Lou," Krieger said. "I think we've got what we wanted from Mr. Rico. We can let him go for now."

Detective Harrell put his glasses back on and looked me up and down.

"Yes, you can go," he said. "But you better watch yourself, Mr. Rico. Like I said, you're the main suspect. We're going to be watching you. You can bet your ass we'll have you back in here again."

"You can watch me all you want," I said, standing up. "I'll be watching, too."

I knew I was being tape recorded or video taped, because as soon as I stood up, as if on cue, the two cops came back in to escort me out.

"Take it easy, Rico," Krieger said to me. I knew he knew I was innocent. The other tec was a different story.

"Yeah," I said, *"cógelo suave."*

⋘ ⋘ ⋘

I couldn't get back to sleep even though I was tired. I just lay in bed thinking about the situation. It looked to me that the same guy who killed Pepito killed the crack head. Or it might have been a group of guys. And now, just because of my greasy hands, I was being suspected. If another body turned up, Krieger and Harrell were going to call me in again. Harrell wanted to nail me. I had to find out who the killer was, not just for Pepito's sake, but for mine. They could put me away no problem when they decided to. And I wasn't too keen on that.

CHAPTER SIX

The Sherman grounds were kept up pretty nice. There were shrub-lined paths between the buildings going up and down hills. The playgrounds had been painted within the last year in nice, bright colors, for the kids to enjoy. Security guards patrolled the grounds on foot and in three-wheelers, and there were security booths by the driveways and overseeing the parking lots.

I was told I could find Noel on the upper level of the main parking lot, facing Broadway. He was washing his black Nissan Altima to the tune of a 2Pac cut. The beeper in the pocket of his baggy pants, the wide gold-link chain around his neck, and the nice car told me right away what was up. He probably didn't have a real job, so the money he got he got dealing.

"You Noel?" I asked as I approached.

He looked up. "Yeah, wassup?"

Noel was shorter than me, about Pepito's height. He had a thin frame but muscular arms. He looked Dominican, with dark-brown skin and closely cut, side-faded hair.

"I'm Tito, Tito Rico," I said. "Pepito was my homey."

Project Death: A Tito Rico Mystery

"Oh, yeah," Noel said, continuing to scrub his car with a soapy rag. The doors were open and the wet floor mats were hanging out. "Dat's crazy, right, what happened?"

"Yeah. You knew him, right?"

"We hung out."

"That's what his sister told me."

"Maritza? She's fly, right?"

"Yeah. You know anything about why Pepito got killed, or who did it?"

Noel dipped the rag in a bucket of water and rang it out.

"Nah," he said.

"You're here, man, you gotta know something."

"Ju'play with fire, ju'get burned, ju'know?"

"What you mean?"

"Ju'snoopin' for the police or what?"

"Nah, nah."

"In the business ju'gotta keep your head up. Ju'get a lot of enemies."

By "business" he meant the drug business. I had never known Pepito to take or deal drugs. The most he ever did, the most any one us in the posse did, was smoke joints. We were around before that sort of thing grew real popular.

"Pepito was dealing?" I asked.

"Hell, yeah."

"How'd he get into that?"

"Why not? How's a man ever going t'get out of dis place?"

"Was that why he got killed?"

Noel threw the rag on the car. He stood facing me.

"Listen, man," he said in Spanish, "I don't know nothing. All I know's that he was dealing. He wanted to get into the business and I helped him out. But he was running his own show."

Noel's beeper went off. He unhooked it and looked at it.

"Ju'better not be wit'da cops," he said.

"I ain't, man," I said.

I began to walk away. Then I heard "Hey!" and turned around.

"Stay away from here," Noel said. "Don't fuck wit' this place."

I nodded my head and kept on walking. Noel obviously wasn't telling me the whole truth. He was hiding something, and seemed afraid to reveal it.

━━◆━ ━◆━ ━◆━

I was going to work the day shift the next week, so Sunday night I met Alonzo at Nig's. We sat at a table by the window. Alonzo had been drinking before I got there, so he was a little tipsy. I could tell by his profanity.

"So you find something?" he asked me over a Colt-45 forty.

"Pepito was dealing."

"Pepito? He was never into that shit."

"I know, but a friend of his got him into the business."

"You think he was killed 'cause'a that?"

"That's what it looks like to me. They found a crack head dead yesterday. The police thinks I did it."

"What?"

I explained to him what had happened.

"That's fucked up!" he said. "Let me get in there wit'ya."

"I still got to find out more."

"I'm itching, man. Ever since I killed that muthafucka, I've been itching to kill some more. It felt good killing that muthafucka."

"You gotta be careful, Alonzo. You don't want to end up in prison again."

"I don't give a fuck."

"What about Roxanne and Moniqua?"

He closed his mouth and spun his bottle so he could read the label.

"I love 'er, Tito. I love that bitch. I met her in prison. She used to come visit her brother every Wednesday. The first time I saw her, I couldn't believe it. I hadn't been with a woman for five years. That's how I got through it, man. Because of her. I was gonna try to escape and kill whoever. But she made me tough it out."

"Roxanne's beautiful."

"Yeah, right? She's all that."

We left Nig's about at about eleven and walked down St. Nicholas. While I was almost drunk, Alonzo was really drunk. He couldn't walk straight, and would have to pause occasionally to get his bearings. We were about to pass a grocery store when Alonzo turned in there and I followed. I figured he wanted to get some beer to take home. The clerk was a black man. He was sitting behind the counter watching a small black and white television. I nodded at him when I came in and went over to pick out a pastry. Alonzo went back to the fridge and pulled out a forty. I could see the clerk looking at Alonzo through the reflection on a large circular mirror he had hanging over the register.

Two women came in laughing loudly. They each bought a pack of cigarettes and left. I looked in the mirror and saw that Alonzo was walking through the aisle to the front with the bottle on his hand. He put the bottle on the counter, and I went to stand next to him with my pastry. As the clerk reached down to pick out a paper back, Alonzo pulled out his gun and jabbed it against the clerk's neck. With his other hand, he pulled him up. I was disoriented enough by the alcohol, and the awkward situation confused me even more.

"What you doing, A?" I hissed.

"Open the register, muthafucka!" Alonzo screamed in the clerk's ear.

The clerk's eyes were bulging out his head. Whispering "Don't, please, don't," he reached a hand over to the register, punched some keys, and opened it. Alonzo let go of the clerk, reached into the drawer, and pulled out bills and food stamps.

"Alonzo, man, what you doing?" I hissed.

"I ain't got no job, man. Ex-con's can't get no job. They always ask you if you've served time. They tell you it don't matter, you still gonna work. That shit is bull."

"I'll give you money."

"Nah. It's Moniqua's birthday next week. Gotta get her something nice."

Alonzo stuck the bills in his pocket.

"You ain't never seen me, muthafucka," he said to the clerk.

Alonzo held the gun pointed at the clerk and backed out. I followed holding the pastry. As soon as Alonzo stepped out, he ran, drunk and all. I looked back at the clerk pulling out a gun from under the counter. That's when I ran, too. I ran not knowing where I was going for several blocks until I got to a park. It was dark in there among the trees, but I didn't care. I just stooped down and threw up because of the exertion. Then I started laughing when I looked at the crushed, stolen pastry I still had in my hand. It had been a long time since I had been involved in something illegal like that.

I felt it was all going to start again.

CHAPTER SEVEN

Ms. Espinoza told me that the Tenants' Association of her building was having a meeting on Wednesday night. I wanted to check it out and maybe get to talk to Mr. Braxton, who had the argument with Pepito the night before he died.

It was hot that day, and so when I arrived home from work, I went out on my fire escape to sit for a while. Some kids had opened the fire hydrant on the corner and were spraying the cars that passed. They teased some drivers, making it look as if they weren't going to spray their cars. So the drivers stupidly attempted to drive through with their windows down. But as soon as they did, the can would appear, and the kids would spray the cars. I laughed as the drivers stuck their heads out to curse.

So engrossed was I in the spectacle below me that I didn't hear my doorbell right away. It was Mircea. She was wearing jeans cut to shorts and a white T-shirt. The first thing she did when I opened the door was put her hands on her hips and look at me defiantly.

Project Death: A Tito Rico Mystery

"Where you been?" she said, and walked in. "You haven't called me or come to see me."

I wanted to put my arms around her, but she didn't let me.

"Get away from me," she said. "When you want it, you think you can get it, right? But you don't care when I want it."

She went to sit on my sofa, but the plastic covering felt uncomfortable to her legs and so she stood right up.

"I'm sorry, baby," I said. "I just haven't had the time. You know I gotta work."

"I work, too," she said, going to look out of my window. Then she climbed out on my fire escape. I went out and stood next to her.

"I'm sorry, Mircea."

She looked down at the kids playing at the pump. Then she turned, wrapped her arms around me, and put her head against my chest.

"You know I miss you, Tito."

"I miss you, too."

She looked up at me so I could kiss her, and I did.

"Tito, I'm sorry about all the bad things I ever said about Pepito."

"That's all right."

"Ever since he got killed, that's been on my mind. You always regret what you thought about somebody when that person dies."

"I know, Mircea. Don't worry about it. What happened happened."

I hadn't told Mircea anything about my own investigation of Pepito's murder. I wanted to keep her out of everything. "You know, I have your money."

I went back into the house and to my bedroom to get her five-hundred dollars.

"Here you go," I said, climbing back out.

Mircea took it back, but hesitantly.

"He never got his money," she said.

"Save it. We're going to need it for the wedding."

Mircea brightened when I said that, and she was about to say something when I kissed her again. I didn't want her to start again on her marriage thing.

◆ ◆ ◆

That night, I put on a nice white shirt and headed down to the projects in my car, which I had finally fixed up. I parked under the elevated track on Broadway and walked down LaSalle Street until I arrived at the building. The Tenants' Association met in a common room on the first floor, next to the elevators. The room was fairly large, but low-ceilinged, with pipes running over people's heads. A fold-up table stood on one side of the room, and the rest was filled with chairs. The people who stood and sat in the room overflowed out into the lobby. I managed to squeeze in through the door and stood pressed by the crowd with my back to the wall.

There were about sixty people present, most of them black. A third were Hispanics, and I could see two white people, a man and a woman. They were white people who had fallen through the cracks in the white establishment, which considered them "white trash." They both looked older than their years, with haggard, ruddy faces and red noses from alcohol consumption. They cheap blue jeans and stained shirts from the local thrift store. I guessed the man was unemployed, or underemployed, as a building porter or dishwasher. The woman, smoking a cigarette, probably took in food stamps like everybody else. I thought, if white people could end up like this, how about blacks and Hispanics who never even get to start?

The meeting had not yet begun when I arrived, so most of the people were involved in conversation with their neighbors. Mrs. Espinosa had told me that there were two or three representatives from each floor in the association. They met once every two weeks, which gave everyone an opportunity to voice complaints or make suggestions about project life that would then be relayed to the Housing Authority. Whether the Housing Authority heeded anything that was said to them was another matter, but at least the people felt that they had a voice.

After about ten minutes, the crowd near the door opened up to allow a large man to enter. He seemed about six feet, with salt-and-pepper hair and beard. He was dressed in a lavender double-breasted suit and wore expensive-looking maroon wingtip shoes. Directly behind him came a cop. I recognized him to be one of the black cops I had noticed the day Pepito was killed and also the time I was talking with Maritza in the park, the one with dark skin, a large mouth and glasses. The men walked over to the table and sat behind it.

The room quieted down as the man in the suit whispered something to the cop and then stood up. He raised a hand and began to talk.

"The Tenants' Association meeting for 23 Lasalle Street will now come to order," he said. "Thank you all for coming. First our secretary will read the minutes from our last meeting."

A black woman near the front stood up and read the minutes. She was wearing blue sweatpants and a sweatshirt and had bright orange curlers in her hair. When she finished, she said, "That's all, Mr. Braxton."

Braxton seemed to be educated and influential, a perfect president for the association.

"Thank you, Alzea," Mr. Braxton continued. "As you all know by now, there have been two very unfortunate occurrences here in our building within the last week."

A murmur of agreement spread through the group. Someone coughed loudly.

"This building is in many ways a haven from the shattered society that surrounds us. We have decent, hardworking people living here, who are trying to live honest lives while they struggle to raise families and rear their children in a good way. Unfortunately, the corrupt elements out there sometimes enter our midst and cause us suffering. Last week, two of our residents were killed. The police are still investigating both cases."

Braxton stopped to look over the crowd.

"Is Mrs. Espinosa here?"

People looked around.

"No, well, we are all grieved at what happened to her son. We are grieved as well at what happened to Mr. Jones."

A few people sucked their teeth in disapproval. Braxton stopped for a moment, but then continued.

"I have with me here someone who is no doubt familiar to many of you, Officer Quinten Neferkara. He is part of the police detail assigned to our building and area. I've asked him to come to speak to us tonight."

Project Death: A Tito Rico Mystery

As the cop stood up, somebody asked, "Where was the police?" Another added, "You all don't do shit."

"You can ask Officer Neferkara questions," Braxton said immediately, "but please do so in an orderly manner."

Neferkara took off his cap.

"Thank you, Mr. Braxton," he said with a slight accent. I guessed he was African. "I know you're all very concerned about what has happened here. But I want to assure you that we are doing all we can to solve these cases and to catch whoever is doing this. Both murders occurred in isolated areas. We obviously can't be everywhere at all times. We have added more policemen to patrol the grounds and will, beginning tomorrow, have officers patrol the building from top to bottom at least three times every night."

"What we supposed to do?" a man asked. "My wife and kids live here with me. What if this's some crazy guy going around killing anybody?"

"We're afraid," an old lady said.

"Like I said," the cop said, "we're increasing security in the building and grounds. But the burden is really on you. Do not open your doors to people unknown to you, be careful when riding the elevators or using the stairs, and make sure to report any suspicious people in the building. You all know who lives here and who doesn't. If you see someone strange, report it to one of your floor representatives."

"What about those white cops you got?" a man asked. "They don't even come in here. I'se seen 'em. They just drive around, don't even get out of their cars."

"That will change. All officers will now begin regular rounds in the building as well as out."

"It's the drugs, man," the only white man in the audience said. "We all know it's the drugs. We should set up some tenants' patrols or something."

"That's not necessary now," Braxton said. "The officers are going to be much more conscientious about their duties. They're all on alert."

"We should still have 'em," the man said. "I'll volunteer."

"That won't be necessary," Braxton said again.

"They got it in other buil..."

"I said," Braxton raised his voice to a menacing level, "that won't be necessary."

The white man shut up and lowered his head. His old lady crossed her legs nervously and took a couple of puffs off her cigarette.

"Well, if there are no other questions, we'll let Officer Neferkara go."

The cop shook Braxton's hand and then made his way through the crowd. He passed right by me but didn't look.

As soon as he stepped out, the crowd started murmuring. Many were saying quite negative things about the cops. But Braxton steered the talk to other matters, namely the social fund, the youth club, and odds and ends like the repair of light fixtures in the hallways.

When the meeting was over, two old women began laying out refreshments on the table. Three men, hoods, gathered around Braxton to talk to him. I waited where I was for a few minutes, then made my way toward Braxton. The three men turned around to look at me as I approached.

"Mr. Braxton," I said, "do you have a minute? Can I talk with you?"

Project Death: A Tito Rico Mystery

Braxton looked at me, perhaps trying to figure out who I was.

"Yes, sure," he said. "Excuse me, I'll be right back."

Braxton separated himself from the three men and moved to the side.

"My name's Tito Rico. I was a friend of Pepito Espinoza, who was killed."

"Oh, yes, I'm very sorry for what happened."

"I was told that you had an argument with him the night before he was murdered."

"What?" Braxton raised his voice.

"You were having an argument with him. I'd like to know what that was about."

"Who told you this?"

"That's not important."

"Listen, Mr. Rico, I've already spoken to the police. Argument? I really don't know what you're talking about. I didn't know the young man at all."

"I'm just trying to figure out what happened to my friend."

"Why don't you let the police do that."

"They've done enough already."

Braxton cleared his throat. "What are you doing here? You're not a tenant."

"Just checking things out."

"I could have you thrown out."

"That won't be necessary," I said. "I'm going."

As soon as I turned to leave, Braxton went back to the three men. I knew they were talking about me, looking at me, or both. I was about to leave the room when I heard a female voice say "Hi" behind me. When I turned, I was looking up at a toast-brown woman with a short, soft, haircut, adorned with curls by each ear. She was wearing tight black pants, a filmy white blouse with see-through sleeves, and a black fishnet sweater over that. He neck was long and covered with a thick, gold necklace. She had a soft round face, round cheeks and a wide smile.

"I've never seen you before," she said. "You just moved in?"

"No, I have a few friends who live here."

"Who?"

"You probably don't know them."

"How'd you like the meeting?"

"Good."

"Yeah, I've been so afraid recently, especially since I live alone."

"You've got to be careful around here."

I was about to leave her.

"You look like you're pretty handy," she said.

"Yeah?"

"I just brought this lock for the inside of my door, but I don't know how to put it on."

I was getting excited. This lady looked to be about my age. She was good-looking to me, too. Black women with short haircuts like her, I like a lot. I didn't know what this lady was up to, but I could feel it.

"You got tools?" I asked.

"Just a hammer."

"I got tools in my car. Where you live?"

"Six B."

Project Death: A Tito Rico Mystery

Somebody put a rough hand on my shoulder. I turned to see the three hoods who were talking with Braxton. They were all about the same height.

"You gotta step, man," one of them said, pointing out the door.

I looked at the woman, who looked confused. I wanted to take a swing at the nearest guy, but controlled myself.

"I'll get the tools," was all I said to the woman and stepped out. I was hot with anger all the way to the car, where I sat for a while until two uptown trains rumbled by overhead. There was nothing that I hated more than to be dissed in front of a girl. With my hand I felt the knife stuck in my belt under my shirt. Like Alonzo, I was itching, too. I knew I was going to use it again sometime.

When I returned to the building with my toolbox in hand, the common room was nearly empty. There was no sign of Braxton or the three hoods. I rode alone in the elevator to the sixth floor and rang the bell at 6B. The latch of the peephole snapped and the woman opened the door. She had taken off the sweater.

"Hi," she said, "come in."

I went inside. She had a studio, and every room was in view from where I stood. A couch was surrounded by a big-ass stereo system and a large floor television. A crib stood in the middle of the living room, a tiny black foot sticking out of the folds of a pink blanket.

"What's your name," I asked.

"Jeraldine, Jeri. That's my little girl Paulette."

"How old is she?"

"Two years."

I looked at her a second, waiting for her to say something.

"Sorry, I'm Tito."

She went to her kitchen table and brought back a new five-inch barrel bolt.

"Here you go. You want anything to drink? I got beer."

"Yeah, get me a beer."

I got to work. With a small hand drill I made some holes in the door and had the bolt on in ten minutes. Jeri tested it herself.

"There you go," I said.

"Thanks, Tito. You want to sit down a while?"

She led me to her couch and I sat with my beer. After checking the baby, Jeri turned on the radio. It was the "quiet storm" hour, so the music was mellow. Then she sat close to me.

It seemed to me that our faces were moving toward each other when the baby started crying. That snapped me out of whatever I was under. I thought of Mircea.

"I gotta go, Jeri."

"No, I'll get her back to sleep."

"Nah, really, I gotta go."

I stood up. I had to leave before my passions got the best of me.

"Let me give you my number," Jeri said. The baby still crying, she hopped to the kitchen table, scribbled her number on a piece of paper, and handed it to me.

"Call me, Tito."

"All right, take it easy," I said, grabbed my tool box and left. As I waited for the elevator, I could still hear the baby crying. I hated it when other women got me going. I promised

Mircea she would be my only while we were together. As for her, I knew she'd never let me down.

CHAPTER EIGHT

I stopped off at a Woolworth's near Yankee Stadium during my lunch hour and picked up some toys for Moniqua. Alonzo told me to stop by for her birthday party Friday night. After work, I took a nap for a few hours, ate two frozen dinners, put on a set of nice clothes, and headed for Alonzo's place.

I could hear the thump-thump of the music as soon as I stepped into the building. The night was warm, and the whole block seemed to be hanging around outside. The door to the apartment was open, and there were people standing outside it, talking, with beers in their hands. I went in and looked around. Roxanne had a one-bedroom apartment with a large living room. There must have been over fifty people in the apartment, dancing, standing against the walls, or sitting down where it was possible. Ribbons in different colors crossed the ceiling. The table was brought just outside the kitchen entrance and covered with soda and beer bottles, cups and paper trays with chips and snacks.

Project Death: A Tito Rico Mystery

Roxanne, with Moniqua on her lap in a yellow dress, was sitting on the couch next to two women who were fussing over the child. I went up to her.

"Hi, Roxanne."

She looked up and smiled, her high cheekbones pushing up her slanted eyes.

"Tito, I'm glad you're here. These are my girlfriends, Joanne and Shandee."

The music was so loud that we were both lipreading more than hearing each other.

"Hi, ladies," I said to the two women. Joanne was quite meaty, with large, round breasts and a short afro. Shandee had wide eyes like an owl's, and her black hair was intricately braided into a criss-crossing pattern.

"What you got?" Roxanne touched the Woolworth's bag.

"For Moniqua."

Roxanne took the bag and helped the eager Moniqua to take out the dolls. The baby seemed very happy.

"What do you say?" Roxanne asked Moniqua.

Moniqua looked up at me shyly, and then smiled, showing no more than four or five pointy teeth. "Tank you."

"Where's Alonzo?"

"He should be back soon. Get something to drink."

I went over to the table and poured myself some Pepsi into a plastic cup. At that moment, Alonzo appeared at the door, followed by Hector. I couldn't believe it. I hadn't seen that homeboy in years. He was from Panama, about my height, and as dark as Alonzo. He had a flat face and a sparse beard that went all the way down his neck. When he saw me, he shook his head and raised his hand.

"Tito-o-o-o-o!"

We slapped hands and hugged.

"Where you been, Hector?"

"Home, man, still up in da Bronx. I got three kids now."

"What you doing?"

"I work for a hardware store, do a little of everything."

"How's María?"

"She's doing good."

"I found the nigger," Alonzo said. "Took a while, but I found the nigger."

"Alonzo told me 'bout Pepo," Hector said to me. "I couldn't believe it."

"He got mixed up with that wack crack," Alonzo said.

"He was dealing?"

"That's what it looks like. I've been trying to find out more about what happened."

"We'll find the sonofabitch," Alonzo said.

Roxanne came up to us with Moniqua and handed her to Alonzo. He kissed her and held her close. I'd never seen Alonzo be so gentle with anything. He held her like a porcelain doll. Alonzo was still crazy, but careful with what was his.

"So what you get her?" I asked Alonzo.

Alonzo smiled. We both began to laugh.

"What's so funny?" Roxanne asked.

"What she needed, Tito: clothes, shoes, this dress."

Unless you go to church all your life, you grow up knowing that not everything's just this or that, black or white. I wasn't entirely sure whether what Alonzo did was right or wrong. That grocery store he robbed wouldn't have to shut down. Nobody really got hurt, and a little girl who needed clothes got what she needed. Where was the crime in that?

Project Death: A Tito Rico Mystery

And if you found your girl knocking boots with a stranger, wouldn't it be right to kill the bastard? People like Alonzo were not immoral. They weren't amoral either. People like Alonzo simply did what needed to be done.

The cake was of pineapple with vanilla ice-cream and pink merengue frosting. It was funny when Moniqua had trouble blowing out the candles. I stayed for an hour or so after the cake was cut, sharing stories with Hector. Alonzo had tried to find Indio and Little Louie, but had no luck. He wanted to get us all together. With Pepito, the posse would have been complete.

I left Alonzo's around eleven. I parked the car down the street from my building and walked up. When I tried to unlock my front door, I actually locked it, which meant that I had left my door open. But I knew I had locked it securely before I left. When I opened my door and turned on my light, I almost shouted in surprise. My place was a wreck. My television was smashed on the floor, my couch and chairs were ripped open, the CD and cassette players were gone. In the kitchen, what had been in my cupboards was on the floor. In my bedroom, all my drawers had been gone through and the clothes in my closet had been pulled off their hangers. Some money I had in the bottom drawer of my dresser was gone.

The only room that was left untouched was the bathroom. I went back into the living room and sat on my wrecked couch for a while with my head in my hands and my arms on my knees. Then I went to check the locks on my door. They didn't seem tampered with. Either the burglar came in through the fire-escape window or was an expert at picking dead bolts. But I always locked the fire-escape window whenever I left the house, and the glass pane was intact. I knew that what I saw around me was not the result of a random burglary. My ransacked home was somehow connected with the project deaths. The only person that came to mind was Braxton. Was he trying to scare me? Was he looking for something? I was already thinking of elaborate theories when I realized that I might be entirely mistaken, like I thought I was with Chimp.

CHAPTER NINE

The Enchilada Man had his bicycle parked in front of Mineo's Pizzeria on Amsterdam. That's how I found him the next morning. He was sitting at the counter having a small cup of espresso. The Enchilada Man was a little man who seemed to appear only in the summertime. He always wore a yellow short-sleeved shirt with pens in the breast pocket, black shorts, white socks, and black shoes. He was painfully thin, with knobby knees and elbows. His sixty-year-old face never seemed shaved or washed, and because he had few teeth, he seemed always to be chewing something, like a rabbit. He spoke no English, except for the expression "Check-it-out!" which he would shout in his high-pitched voice while riding his ancient bicycle around the neighborhood. Attached to the front of the bicycle was a metal basket where he kept warm the enchiladas which he sold for a dollar each. That was how he made his living, selling enchiladas. I had one or two on occasion, and they were really good.

"Hey, *amigo*, how's it going?" I asked him in Spanish.

"Tito, you want an enchilada?" he asked eagerly.

"Yeah, let me get one."

He drained his cup and went out to his bicycle. I followed him with a dollar in my hand.

"You ride all around here, don't you?" I asked.

"Yes, I go everywhere."

"You ever ride down by 125th?"

"Sometimes."

He handed me the enchilada and I gave him the dollar.

"How'd you like to make some extra money?"

His face brightened up.

"Yes, how?"

"You know those projects down by 125th?"

"Yes."

"I want you to ride around there, sell your enchiladas for a couple of days. I want you to watch, that's all. Just watch what goes on. I want you especially to watch what goes on around a particular building."

I gave him the number of Pepito's building.

"There are policemen who work there. I want you to watch them, too. I want to know if you see them doing anything strange."

"Like what, Tito?"

"You'll know, I think. Here's twenty dollars."

I took out a twenty-dollar bill and handed it to him. He stuck it deep in his pocket.

"You come by the pizzeria a lot, don't you?"

"Yes, to have my coffee."

"I'll probably see you here soon. You tell me what you see. Understand?"

He smiled and nodded his head eagerly.

"I always understand money," he said.

Project Death: A Tito Rico Mystery

He pushed his bike and nimbly jumped on the seat. He rode away yelling, "Check-it-out! Check-it-out!" I had the feeling I had thrown away good money.

⋙⋙⋙⋙⋙

I spent most of the day cleaning up the mess in my apartment. I didn't call the police about it because I knew that it would not have done any good. They would have sent one or two cops over, who would have asked me some inane questions, jotted down useless information, told me they would look into it and then disappear. Had something like this happened on the Upper East Side, the SWAT team would have blanketed the area. But this was Washington Heights, the Dominican drug center of New York. Anything less than one of their own getting shot up here was considered trivial by the police.

I was a little scared now. If I had been at home sleeping, something worse could have happened. I could've been killed. So I went to the local hardware store and brought a jimmy-proof double-key deadbolt. After an hour of trying I was able to fit it and make it work. That type of lock was harder to pick because the mechanism inside was more complicated. It was expensive, but I wanted to be safe.

I called Alonzo, but there was nobody home. That was strange, because I knew Alonzo was going to get drunk at the party and he would be at home the next day sleeping it off.

What I wanted was a gun, and Alonzo could find me one cheap.

I was going to stay home Saturday night, just in case my buddies came back, but then I got an idea. I wanted to check out the projects at night. I put on a black windbreaker, black sneakers, and a baseball cap, which I pulled low over my eyes. Then I went out, bought a newspaper, drove down and parked on LaSalle Street, as close as possible to Pepito's building as I could get. Shifting over to the passenger's seat, I made believe I was reading the paper while I kept an eye on the front of the building and on the people going up and down the block. There was a pay phone near the car, which got a lot of attention from both men and women, most of them answering beeper calls. Most of the windows in the building were wide open and lit, and I could hear music coming from several directions. Since the night was nice, there were kids playing in the playgrounds and people sitting on the benches in front of the building. At one point, somewhere behind me, I heard a bottle crash, a scream, then laughter. A group of kids came running up the block. Young black women, looking good enough to eat in tight shorts and revealing tops, walked past men who shimmied and macked. Black people played the game better than anybody. The men were clever and knew what to say; the women knew how to look and how to respond.

After two hours, I was getting tired. I got out of my car, walked to a grocery store on the corner of 125th and Broadway, and bought a beer. Then I cut through the grounds and arrived in front of Pepito's building. I sat down on a bench with my back to the playground, and kept my eyes on the entrance of the building as I drank my beer. Before I got up and walked into the lobby, I saw drugs exchange hands four times. Twice, it happened fast. Two or three guys walking past each other, one handing over money, the other handing over a few vials. Twice, they stood around, looking around nervously, counting cash, checking the crack in the vials in the light over the door.

After I finished my beer, I walked into the lobby. The door to the stairwell was open and there were about ten guys, blacks and Hispanics, hanging out in the stairwell. I glanced at them as I came in, then turned to some notices near the mailboxes and read them.

The gang, formerly laughing, grew silent. I could see, out of the corner of my eye, one of them was approaching me.

"Ju'looking foh some shit? I got it," I heard.

I turned and faced Noel. He didn't recognize me right away. He thought I was looking to buy some drugs. Behind him, the rest of the gang was looking at me.

"Nah, man," I said, and turned away, but Noel grabbed my hat by the brim and pulled it off my head.

"I tol ju not t'come 'round here!" he yelled, stepping back to avoid my swinging arm as I tried to grab my hat back.

"Yo," he yelled back to his friends, "he's wit' d'cops!"

"I'm not, man!" I yelled as the gang came out of the stairwell and stood behind Noel. I began to back out.

"Noel, I ain't with the cops."

One of their number, a tall, skinny black kid about sixteen-years old, raised up the front of his sweatshirt and began to draw out a black object. I didn't stay long enough to find out if it was a gun or not. I turned on my heels and ran out the door. But they ran after me, yelling. I didn't run toward my car, knowing that I would not have the time to reach it, jump in, and drive off, before the gang was on me. So I cut across the lawn, jumped over a short fence, and ran deeper into the projects, veering to my left. That may have been a mistake, but I didn't care. I ran up a set of steps to a higher level, for some of the buildings were built higher up on hills, crossed another lawn, and almost broke my foot jumping over a low brick rampart onto the hood of a car in a parking lot below. For a second, I was out of sight of the gang, but I could hear them shouting. I moved in among the cars, ducking down just in time behind an Oldsmobile as a series of feet hammered down on car hoods.

"Muthafucka's here somewhere!" I heard one of them say.

Keeping low, I snaked my way among some more cars, occasionally looking under the cars at the encroaching feet of my pursuers. It had been a long time since I had been so scared. My heart was beating so hard, and the blood was gushing so much around my head, that I felt a stroke was going to come upon me at any moment. I wasn't sure where I was, or how far I was from an exit. But I kept on moving.

The sweep of a moving headlight passed behind me. A car began entering the lot. I craned my neck just enough to see that it was a project security car. I was so glad that I stood up and began running toward it. The black guard who was driving opened the door quickly and stepped out, a gun pointed at me. It was then that I noticed that the gang was nowhere to be found. I stopped running.

"What you doing? You live here?" he yelled out.

I looked around again, to make sure Noel and his boys weren't hiding anywhere.

"Nah, nah, chill!" I yelled back, my hands up.

"Get moving! If I see you back here again, I'll call the police."

Project Death: A Tito Rico Mystery

"All right, all right!" I said, moving toward the exit of the lot, which went out to 125th Street. I crossed the street and made believe I was making a call at a pay phone right outside a video rental store. I watched the patrol car drive around the lot, come out, and then turn the corner onto Amsterdam.

I stayed at the phone a few minutes, looking for any sign of Noel and his boys. But they were gone. I walked down Amsterdam until I reached another parking lot, cut through there, and got back to my car parked on LaSalle. It was past midnight when I arrived home and found everything in order. I felt a little calmer than I was an hour before when I had ten guys running after me wanting to kill me. But I was scared. The situation was getting out of hand. Noel was after me. Somebody else, breaking into my apartment, was after me. I needed a gun, fast. And I couldn't run. That's not what my father would have done. The third day after arriving in this country, he was held up by two black guys who took his money and cut his arm. From that day, he always carried a large bowie knife in his belt. And nobody else ever held him up again.

CHAPTER TEN

In the morning I went out to a local *bodega* and bought
me a ham sandwich and a Yoo-hoo. That was my breakfast.
For most of the morning I sat by the window and listened to
the radio. But there was more noise coming from outside.
Summertime is a great time to live in the *barrio*. Everybody
seems so much happier and carefree. Men stand by the curbs
sipping beer in paper bags, and old men in straw hats or fedo-
ras set up rickety tables on the corners to play dominoes.
Every other fire hydrant is open and wetting everything in
sight. Young girls, thirteen and fourteen, dress up and make
themselves up so they look eighteen. That always kills me. I
get all excited looking at a girl sometimes, and then I realize
that despite all the makeup and the tight clothes, she's probably in junior high. But that doesn't mean anything. By the
time she's halfway through high school, she'll probably get
pregnant. Kids start out too young these days, boys and girls.
I heard on the radio that most girls have sex by the time
they're fifteen, but when asked about it, wished that they had
waited until they were seventeen. Big difference. When I was

that age, though, I didn't care either. But now that I'm older, I wouldn't want my fifteen-year-old daughter sleeping around with guys who wear pants three times their size and think they look good in them.

I must have dozed off because around noon, I was startled by a heavy knock on my door. When I went to see who it was, I couldn't see anybody through the peephole. I thought that maybe I was hearing things. I went back to sit by the window and heard more knocking. When I looked through the peephole again, I still couldn't see anybody.

"Who is it?" I yelled through the door.

No answer. But I knew there was somebody there. Without thinking, I angrily opened the door, ready to confront whoever was playing with me. A big black man in a black t-shirt and a jean survival vest pushed me into my apartment. I almost fell backward, but held my ground and put my arms up, ready to fight. Another black man, about as big as him, stepped inside. Finally, Chimp, in a cream-colored suit, black shirt open at the neck, and a charcoal, feathered pimp hat, came in. He looked around and then closed the door gently.

"You're Tito, right?" Chimp said as he walked around the room, looking at some of the pictures I have on my wall. He stopped at a picture of Mircea. The glass of the frame, over Mircea's face, was cracked when my apartment was wrecked. All my pictures had been thrown on the floor.

Chimp glanced over at me with a smile. He pulled the cardboard back of the frame out and took out the large photo. Mircea was sitting by a fountain, her head and hair thrown back, a smile on her face.

"Pretty lady," Chimp said. "Sister?"

"My girl," I said through clenched teeth.

Chimp took the picture to the sofa and sat down. After looking at it a moment longer, he looked back at me.

"What you want?" I asked him.

"I'm looking for a friend of yours, Alonzo Brown."

I looked at his two men. They both had rock-hard faces and big arms. One of them was wearing shades and had an unmoving toothpick coming out of the side of his mouth. They may have been the men who were with him at his booking joint, but I wasn't sure.

"I'm'a call the cops!" I said.

One of the men saw my phone hanging on the wall over my table. He walked over to it and ripped it off the wall with one hand.

"Where's your homey?" Chimp asked. His lower lip stuck out in a pouting, mocking manner.

"I don't know."

"Somebody recognized him when you two came to my place and showed me disrespect. You don't go into a man's place and disrespect him. No, no. That's the last thing you'll ever want to do."

One of the men came toward me. I turned and gave him a right cut to the side of his face. He didn't flinch. He swung at me, but I ducked and belted him near the groin. That stopped him a moment. But the other guy was already behind me. He put me in a headlock and gave me the hardest punch in the face I have ever received. Whether he let me go purposely or not, I couldn't tell, but in the next moment I was sitting on the floor and blood was running like water from my nose down my chest. My eyes were so watery that the people around me turned into shapeless, dark forms. I was picked up roughly and thrown against the couch.

Chimp was in front of me. The man in the vest pulled out a gun and cocked it next to my head.

"Where's your friend?" Chimp asked me, leaning down so that his face was in front of mine.

"I told you, I don't know."

"Am I your bitch?"

"What?"

"You heard me, am I your bitch?"

"Nah, man."

"Then why you fuckin with me?"

"I ain't fuckin. I don't know."

"Listen, man, my beef's not with you. It's with your friend. So just tell me where I can find him and everything'll be all right."

I felt the gun press tighter against my temple. Somebody told me you never hear the bang. But I was waiting for it.

"All right, I'll tell you," I said.

I made up some address.

"That's good," Chimp said, standing up straight. "You see, we ain't gonna kill you. You saved my life. I remember that. It's your buddy I want."

He leaned in again suddenly.

"But I tell you one thing. If you lied to me, we're coming back, and then we're gonna kill you."

The man with the gun put his piece away. The other man went to the door and opened it.

"You thought I killed your buddy?" Chimp asked. "Like I told you before, I had nothing to do with that. But if you're still looking, check out Dixie's Lounge tonight. Something's going down."

Chimp took out a cigarette from the inside pocket of his suit jacket and lit it in his mouth. Then he stepped out, followed by his two boys. When I was alone, I went into the bathroom and washed my face. The blood hadn't stopped yet so I sat quietly on the toilet holding a wash rag against my nose, counting the minutes. Chimp would be back, and I didn't want to be there. As soon as the blood stopped, I got my gym bag, threw in some clothes, and left, locking all my locks.

CHAPTER ELEVEN

The first thing I did was go down to a pay phone on the corner and try to call Alonzo to tell him about Chimp. But there was nobody home. I needed to be somewhere else for a while, or until I checked out Dixie's Lounge that night. I wasn't sure why Chimp had told me about it. Did he know who killed Pepito? But I couldn't pass it up. I was going for whatever information I could get. And since I now had more people after me than I could count, I had to get everything solved fast, or it would be the end of Tito Rico. I dialed information, too, and got the address of the only Dixie's Lounge listed, one on 125th, near Madison Avenue.

I went over to Mineo's pizzeria and asked about the Enchilada Man, but nobody had seen him yet. After a soda and a slice, I took the C train down to Central Park. I got off at 72nd Street and I walked into Central Park and over to the Cherry Hill Fountain across from the big lake. I sat on the steps leading down to the concourse and watched the people roller blade. When I got tired of that, I went over to the lake. There was a solitary spot near the water that I had discovered when I was a kid. You had to go down an incline of brambles, skip across some rocks and climb over a large bush. Behind the bush was a grassy clearing about five feet square, shadowed by two maple trees and surrounded by a steep descent. The only view from that spot was a small, overgrown island about twenty feet from the shore and the bridge that cuts the lake in the middle. This spot, Tito's Point, saw a lot of me in my younger days. I used to go here a lot whenever anything serious was bothering me. Even though I was in the middle of the city, being in that spot made me think I was alone in some wilderness. And it seems that when there are problems, the best thing to do is get away and be alone. Forget about talking to somebody. That hardly ever works. You just have to grit your teeth and think it out. All by yourself. That's because nobody ever really understands your problems. They can't get into your head. From what I remembered, Jesus did the same thing. He used to go into the wilderness to pray and fast. And if Jesus had to do it, there was no other choice for a nobody like me.

A woman and her daughter rowed their boat near my spot. They looked wealthy, from their blonde hair, their golden tans and their crisp white clothing. The daughter was the first to notice me and pointed me out to her mother. She looked, and I blew a kiss at her. The mother made like I wasn't there, but rowed out of there as quick as she could. After that, I placed my bag under my head and lay back as best as I could. All I could hear was the lapping of the water, and voices, voices all around me. People talking and laughing. But in the cool breeze, shaded by the trees, I fell asleep.

Project Death: A Tito Rico Mystery

⊸⊷⊸ ⊸⊷⊸ ⊸⊷⊸

Dixie's Lounge was next to a beauty salon with a front window covered with photographs of clients with their new hairstyles. The styles went from ultra-short bobs to complicated, multi-layered African weaves. I noticed the pictures as I stood outside the bar making up my mind whether to go in or not.

The name of the lounge was in blue neon above the door and in white neon in the dark windows. The inside was spacious. A rectangular bar stood in the middle of the room, with a piano next to it, coming off a corner. Inside the rectangular bar was a small stage rising above the glasses, bottles and taps. A microphone stand and a microphone stood on the stage. Round tables filled up the rest of the space. There weren't many people at the bar, but most of the tables were occupied. I went to sit at the bar, by the piano. The bartender noticed me right away and came to ask what I wanted. As far as I could tell, I was the only non-black person I could see. But I knew that if I stayed quiet and minded my own business, nobody would bother me.

I arrived at the bar at nine. By ten, I had finished two Colt-45's and two Heinekens. I didn't know what I was waiting for. I kept my eyes open for anybody I knew, but I didn't know anybody. When the pay phone by the restrooms was free, I went and called Alonzo, but there was still no answer. After I returned to my stool, a very thin man with long side burns, a patchwork suit that was forty-years old, and a pork-pie hat was sitting at the piano. He began to finger the keys, and played something bluesy. Then a woman in a short black, shoulderless dress climbed on the stage and took the microphone off the stand. The bartender lowered the stand. There was something familiar about the woman, and I stared until I realized it was Jeri, the woman I had met after the tenants' meeting at the projects.

Many of the patrons were turning their chairs to face Jeri. Those at the bar beside and around her crowded to the side of the bar she was facing. I couldn't move anymore because the piano was next to me.

"How's everybody tonight?" Jeri asked. "Everybody's looking so good."

A man at a table waved at Jeri.

"Hi," she acknowledged. "I'm going to start off tonight with an old standard some of you may know. It's something Billie Holiday used to do..."

Some applause stopped her.

"That's right. We all love Lady Day. She started it all. Without her, I wouldn't be here. The song's called 'Big Stuff.'"

The pianist began to play, and Jeri began to sing. I'd never heard the song before, but Jeri did a good job, especially when she snarled her voice for the refrains. She sang several more songs, and then stopped for a break. Before she climbed down from the stage, I called her name. She looked around, unsure of who was calling her name, and then saw me. With a surprised expression, she came over to me.

"How'd you know I was here?" she asked.

"I didn't. I just came by. You didn't tell me you were a singer."

Jeri smiled widely, making her round face look even rounder. Her forehead and the sides of her face glistened with sweat.

"I do it a few nights a week. Some extra money."

"You're pretty good. Where'd you learn how to sing?"

"Down in Virginia, where I grew up. I used to sing in the choir, at church."

She placed her arms akimbo and became serious.

"You haven't called me."

"I've been busy. But I was gonna."

"Tell me another one," she said, but smiled again. "You know, I was serious about that."

The door of the bar flew open and about twenty cops poured in, guns drawn. Jeri was so startled at the sudden noise that she knocked my bottles off the bar. Then she held on to me in fright.

"Police! Nobody move! Everybody stay where you are!" one of the cops kept repeating while he gave out orders to the others. Some of the cops went toward the back of the lounge.

I felt somebody grab my arm. It was the bartender. He was a pudgy, reddish-brown man, with a thick black moustache and a receding hairline. His bulging eyes were trained on me.

"Get 'er out o' heah!" he whispered, referring to Jeri. "She don't got nuthin' to do wit' this."

I pulled my arm from him as a bottle crashed near the rear of the lounge. Gunshots began to ring, and I took Jeri to the ground. Everybody scattered. Tables were knocked over, glasses were flying, more shots were fired. I couldn't tell exactly what was happening because I was trying to stay low. Holding on to Jeri, I went around the corner of the bar, knocking the stools aside to stick as close to the wood as possible.

"This way!" Jeri said to me, and began to pull me. For a second, I looked up and saw what was happening clear as crystal. It was a moment of enlightenment, when all the action around me seemed to freeze long enough for me to appreciate every detail. Most of the people were trying to run toward the exit. Some men were wrestling with the cops. Two men jumped over the bar top to take refuge behind the bar. I saw a tall man in a blue-green suit with a gun in his hand. He was firing this way and that without aiming. Two women were cowering between a cigarette machine and a corner of the lounge. One man was lying face down by the pay phone. The receiver was dangling over his head.

Jeri pulled me along the edge of the bar, and we turned another corner of it. Then we made toward a curtained doorway and passed into a dark, narrow hallway with doors to each side. At the end of the hallway was a rusty door with a red exit sign over it. The lock was stiff, but I shouldered the door and it opened out into an alley of uneven, littered ground with large puddles of water. We began to run to our left, but Jeri had to stop because of her heels. She took them off and ran in stockinged feet. I was worried that she'd get a piece of glass stuck in her foot. We were approaching another alley that crossed the one we were in when we heard: "I want everything you got! Give it up, or you're dead!"

Then a slap and a grunt.

We slowed down and put our backs to the brick wall under a fire escape and next to a large trash receptacle. I touched Jeri's arm to make her stay where she was and then I slid along the wall to the corner of the intersection of the other alley. I put out my head just enough to see what was happening.

Project Death: A Tito Rico Mystery

Two cops were pressing a black man against the wall. Both cops looked Hispanic. One had his stick out, the end pressed under the man's neck. The other had his revolver by his hip. The man was dressed in a green T-shirt and had a baseball cap backwards on his head.

The man reached under his shirt and took out a white paper bag. The cop with the stick snatched it from him, put his stick in his belt, and checked the bag.

"You tell Reedy we want four hundred a week, you got that, nigger?"

"Yeah, yeah!"

The other cop snatched the hat from the man and threw it to the ground.

"Fuckin nigger," he said, and pushed him against the wall.

I slid back to Jeri.

"Come on," I said, and we began to walk slowly back in the direction we had come. Then we broke into a sprint, went down another alley, and came to a narrow passage blocked by a gate. I moved a garbage can next to the gate and climbed over. Then I helped Jeri climb over. We came out on a small street across from Marcus Garvey Park.

"Put on your shoes," I said.

Jeri held up her feet, and she was splattered in mud to the knees. We crossed the street, entered the park, and on the other side of it sat down on a bench. We could hear the wail of a siren.

"Tito, I'm so scared," she said, putting her arms around me. I could smell the perspiration under her armpits.

"Just be cool for a while."

"Did you have anything to do with this?"

"I don't know."

"At the meeting, those men wanted to throw you out. What's going on? Who are you?"

A short, thin, black man in baggy clothes approached us. I fisted my hands.

"Smoke? Smoke?" he said to me, while looking at Jeri.

"Nope," I said.

He walked on, keeping his eyes on Jeri.

"What did you see back there?" Jeri asked me.

"Just two cops shaking down a drug dealer."

"Was that why they busted Dixie's?"

"I guess. Do they deal there?"

Jeri didn't say anything.

"You know anybody named Reedy?"

"Yes," Jeri said. "He owns Dixie's."

The park was so small you could see across it. Two police cars stopped on the other side of the park, leaving their chase lights spinning and causing the trees to be illuminated on and off.

"We'd better go," I said.

We walked to Fifth Avenue and stopped a cab. I told the driver to take us to the projects, but made him first go south, then west. He went up Broadway, then down Lasalle, where he dropped us off.

Jeri thought I was coming with her, but I didn't want to risk seeing Noel and his friends again.

"But I'm scared, Tito. What if they come get me?"

"Who? The police?"

"The police, the drug dealers, all of them. They know I sing at that club."

"Who's Reedy? The bartender?"

Project Death: A Tito Rico Mystery

"Yes."

"Did he have you on his books?"

"No, he just paid me cash, plus the tips."

"Then I don't think you have to worry, Jeri."

"Tito, please stay with me."

She was looking at me with her eyes wide. I thought she was going to start crying.

"Jeri, I gotta go. I'll call you, I promise. I just don't want you to get mixed up in any of this."

"In what?"

"I'll explain sometime, but I gotta go now."

I left Jeri and walked up toward Broadway. When I got to the corner, I almost jumped. I had left my gym bag at Dixie's. My wallet was in my pocket, but my house keys were in that bag. I thought hard about what I had in that bag, but there was nothing that would lead the police to me if they happened to pick it up. So there was no way that I could get back into my apartment. I turned back to see if I could see Jeri, but she had walked home.

There was no place else to go but back to Jeri. I crossed the street and walked slowly to the projects, keeping my eyes open wide for any sign of Noel. I wasn't up for another chase. There was a gang sitting on the benches by the playground outside the building, but they weren't the same gang from before. The lobby was empty except for a Hispanic man and woman who were talking.

"Tito," Jeri said as she opened her door. But she didn't open it wide.

"I left my keys at the lounge," I said. "I can't get back into my place."

Jeri let me in. Her baby was sleeping in the crib in the living room.

"You leave her here alone when you go sing?" I asked.

"Who else am I going to leave her with?" Jeri said, suddenly angry. She went into the kitchen. I watched her as she took some bread off the refrigerator, slapped it down on her counter, made a peanut butter and jelly sandwich, took a glass from the cupboard, washed it, dried it, took a container of juice from the refrigerator, poured some juice. She did all this angrily. Then she brought the sandwich and the juice to me and pushed it into my hands.

Jeri went to check on her baby. I put the sandwich and the juice down on a small table, went to Jeri, put my hands on her waist, and turned her around to face me. She had on a lot of foundation, which made her skin look flawless, except for where perspiration had wrinkled the makeup film. Then I kissed her for a long time. Her mouth was bigger than Mircea's, so I had a hard time keeping my lips outside of her's. But I didn't mind when it was my mouth that was inside.

I stayed with Jeri that night and went to work the next morning with the same clothes I had on the day before. It was a good thing we had uniforms at work.

CHAPTER TWELVE

I met Alonzo after work in a tiny, corner diner on 149th and Broadway. It was basically one long counter with about ten stools. Those who couldn't sit at the counter could stand across from it and look out the window while they ate. They specialized in Cuban sandwiches and coffee, milk shakes and stuffed potatoes. Those were my favorites and I always had a couple when I passed that diner. You could have them stuffed with pork or beef. The owner was a tough, old character who had opposed Castro after the revolution. He had been tortured and put in prison for ten years. The topic of conversation at the diner was always something about Cuba or Castro, and it seemed I saw the same old men at the place all the time.

I told Alonzo all about Chimp. He seemed mad.

"I gave him a wrong address and then left the house," I said. "I haven't been back there since yesterday."

"He don't know where I live, but I know where he is," Alonzo said with a cruel gleam in his eye. I knew what that meant.

"Alonzo, we gotta lay low. We can't do anything to him yet. Didn't he tell me to check out that bar? He told me that if I wanted to find out what happened to Pepo, I should check out that bar. Maybe he knows more."

"If he hurts my family..."

"But who else knows where you live?"

"Not too many people."

"So I think you'll be all right."

Alonzo stared at me a moment and wrinkled his brow in puzzlement.

"Chimp told you somebody recognized me. But how come he knew where *you* lived?"

That question had crossed my mind before. I couldn't figure it out either.

"I don't know, Alonzo, I don't know. What I'm worried about is that I can't go back to my place. I can't stay there anymore. Chimp said he was coming back to kill me if he couldn't find you."

The old men sitting next to us were having a heated discussion about the possibility of overthrowing Castro by a popular revolt. The consensus was in the negative. Castro's system of civilian spies was too well entrenched to allow the possibility of some grass-roots movement against him.

"You gotta find someplace else to live in the meantime," Alonzo said. "Roxanne's place is too small, so I can't offer you that. Anyway, I don't want her and the baby to get mixed up in any of this. They don't know anything."

"I know what you mean."

"But you need to get back into your place to get your stuff. Let me call Hector. He does locks."

Project Death: A Tito Rico Mystery

Hector met us at my place with a bag full of tools. It took about an hour, but he ended up jimmying my new jimmy-proof lock and picking the others. When we got inside, we sat around and drank some beers. Hector had brought a *Daily News* with him. He handed it to me and I looked it over.

"Look at this," I said to Alonzo.

He came over to me and glanced over the small article on page twenty-two that I was pointing at:

NEW YORK—An unidentified nineteen-year-old black male was found beaten and stabbed multiple times yesterday in an abandoned lot off 125th Street near the Sherman projects of Harlem. He was taken to Columbia-Presbyterian Hospital and was listed in critical condition.

"You think that has anything to do with Pepo?" Alonzo asked.

"I don't know, but I got a friend who works in that hospital. I'm going to try and get in there to talk to this guy."

"You guys turning into detectives?" Hector said with a laugh.

"That's right," Alonzo said seriously. "And you're joining us."

"What, to try to find out what happened to Pepo?"

"That's right."

"Then I guess," Hector said, raising his Bud, "the posse's back in action."

We drank to that. We knew we would need Hector's help again.

CHAPTER THIRTEEN

I needed a place to stay fast, and so Alonzo took me to a tiny hotel in Harlem down the block from Sylvia's soul-food restaurant. It was in a narrow brownstone in a street of narrow, run-down, drab-looking brownstones, every other one of which was burned out or condemned. I imagined that sixty years before, during Harlem's hey-day, those brownstones all looked nice. It was a shame there was nothing to be proud of anymore.

The hotel was called the New Orleans Claire View and only charged fifteen a night for a room the size of a closet. The proprietor was a hunchbacked, toothless old man who had trouble reaching for the room key on the peg behind him. My room was on the second landing, and as we were climbing up, we met a drugged-out man who looked like he was going to topple down on us. He kept asking us for a quarter. Alonzo wanted to push him down the stairs, but I gave him two quarters and he was happy.

The brownstone had obviously been a private residence in better days. To make money, every room was closed off into individual units. There was a strong smell of marijuana everywhere. My room had no doorknob and was secured by a padlock.

The room wasn't larger than a typical jail cell. A small bed stood under a curtainless window of cracked glass. A dresser with two drawers missing was behind the door. On a hook on the wall was somebody's black ski cap. The bathroom, we discovered, was down the hall and was meant to be shared by all the tenants on the floor.

I jumped on the bed. Surprisingly, it was comfortable enough, and I could feel no lumps or misplaced springs.

"What else you gonna get for fi'teen dollars a night?" Alonzo asked me, looking into the drawers of my dresser. He found a *Blacktail* magazine and paged through it.

"How long you planning on staying here?"

"I don't know. Until this is all over."

"Tito, let's go see Chimp again. I'll kill him. That'll end our problems."

"Nah, that won't help. That'll only make it worse. It looks like he's got juice."

I thought of Chimp's two boys and the feel of that gun against my head. I hated having guns pressed against my head. Alonzo used to do it, playing around, trying to show off, and I always hated it.

Alonzo told me to hang tight for a few hours. He was going to come back with a gun for me. When he left, I lay back in the bed and looked up at the sky through the dirty window. It was a summer night, bright blue, and a star would occasionally wink at me. I tried to remember what happened in the alley behind Dixie's. Two cops were shaking down a drug dealer. I saw one cop take a bag of something, probably cocaine or heroine, from the dealer and stuff it in his shirt. He was also demanding protection money. Was the raid a concerted event, to serve as a warning, or were those two rogue cops taking advantage of the situation to serve their own ends? It couldn't be that all those cops in the raid were in on the racket. It was no big news that there were corrupt cops who extorted money from dealers. But there couldn't be more than a handful in a precinct, could there? Two years before, about five cops had made the front pages when they were busted for corruption in a Bronx precinct. The police commissioner held a press conference and threw their badges down on a table. He said no cop would ever have to wear those same tainted shields again. I began to wonder if I was getting mixed up in something similar.

Alonzo came back with a .38 for me. The only other gun I ever had was a cheap little .22 I wore for a while when I was brasher and younger. I came to see that guns caused more problems than they could fix. But I was changing my mind, and I knew I couldn't walk around anymore without one.

CHAPTER FOURTEEN

There were days that Slatum Turner worked the same line that I did. We would ride together until 149th Street, and then he would switch to the 2 train and continue up alone. He was a slow man, slow looking, slow speaking and slow moving. I thought he was retarded the first time I met him, but then I realized he was quite intelligent. He had earned a Bachelor's degree in English from Lehman College in the '70's. He was about fifty and still lived with his mother. I felt sorry for Slatum most of the time. I pictured myself in his place sometimes, and wondered if he ever got lonely.

The train had just pulled out of the 125th Street stop, and so we were alone in the station, sweeping the floor. I began to joke with Slatum again, telling him that one of the token-booth clerks, Wilfrida James, was making eyes at him. He always smiled and shook his head, but for the first time, it seemed he was actually taking me seriously.

"You saw her, Tito?" Slatum asked me slowly, as if being careful about the words he was choosing.

None of it was true, but I played along. "Yeah, sure. Every time we go into her station, she can't keep her eyes off of you."

"How come I've never seen her?"

"Sure, you're not gonna see her. Women don't make it obvious they're looking, like men do. A guy never knows a woman is scoping him out."

"You sure, Tito?" he asked me again, stopping and leaning over the top of his push-broom. He was looking down into the tracks, daydreaming. He was probably imagining visiting Wilfrida with flowers and candy in his hands.

"Slatum, you know I'm just playing with you," I said, feeling bad that I was adding to his delusion. But he didn't hear me. Some people were entering the platform after making the turnstiles crackle.

"What you say, Tito?"

He looked over at me, and I looked over at the light deep in the tunnel. The train was coming. I looked at my watch.

"We'd better finish up and get on this train," I said.

There were about a dozen people waiting for the train. One man was leaning against the wall reading a newspaper. He was wearing a gray pullover, a baseball cap, and sunglasses. When I glanced in his direction, he turned his head sharply back to his paper.

When the train came, Slatum and I got on with our black garbage bags. We sat down across from each other without talking. I just looked up and read the advertisements. I liked reading this on-going Spanish comic strip about AIDS. It was up to the fifth installment. The main guy found out he had AIDS in the last installment, and was worried that he would lose his girlfriend. That made me think of

Mircea. She even looked like the lady in the comic strip. I had to give her a call sometime soon.

Slatum got off at 149th Street. But before he did, he asked me again if I was sure that Wilfrida James was making eyes at him. I just smiled and waved my hand in front of his face. That was supposed to mean that I was only kidding, but it didn't seem to register that way for Slatum. His face beamed and his large cheeks blushed. As he got off the train, it looked like he was floating on air.

The train came out of the bowels of the earth and became elevated. The afternoon sun sent shifting waves of blinding light as the train wound its way through the buildings. I stayed on a few stops until 176th Street. There I got off and went to the railing to look out over the Bronx until the people had cleared the platform. I then walked to the end of the platform and began to sweep, pouring the garbage from the dustpan into my garbage bag. I was near the stairs when I noticed that the black man in the gray pullover was sitting on the benches by the stairs, reading his paper. Another train came and went, people boarded and exited, and he did not move. I noticed him, but at the moment didn't feel anything amiss, like when you notice a cockroach crawling across your ceiling and don't worry about it because you can't reach the cockroach anyway. I continued sweeping all the way to the stairs and then began to descend the steps, pulling my garbage bag, which was becoming filled, behind me. When I was halfway down the stairs, I heard some heavy steps behind me. I looked up to see the black man rushing down the stairs toward me. He reached under his pullover and pulled out a silver gun. I swung the garbage bag at him and bounded down the rest of the steps, three at a time. A man and a woman were beginning to climb the steps, and the woman gave out a scream as I pushed her aside.

When I reached the bottom, the landing where the turnstiles were, I realized that I still had my broom in my hand. Instead of darting from the steps, I swung under them, and then rebounded, swinging the tip of my broom toward the man's face. As soon as I felt the impact, I let go, and ran toward the turnstiles. As I jumped over them, a shot hit the glass of the token booth directly in front of me, causing a star-shaped figure, but not breaking the glass. The token clerk looked behind me with wide eyes, and then disappeared as he ducked. I could still hear the woman screaming, and a man yelling "Hey! Hey!" But I didn't look back. As I ran toward the steps that led to the street, another shot hit the wood floor near my feet, causing a neat hole. As I was about to go down the first step, I was struck from behind and propelled forward. I rolled down the stairs fighting the man. With one hand, I kept his gun pointed away from me, and with the other I grabbed his throat. I knew I was getting hurt bad rolling down the steps, but I couldn't feel it because I was intent on staying alive and not letting this man kill me. Every time he rolled underneath me, I made sure to ram his head against the steps.

The gun flew out of his hand and clanged down the steps. When we reached the bottom, we both began to struggle for the gun, which had fallen behind the wheel of a parked car. I jumped for it, but he kicked me aside. He went for it, but I knocked him down. That was my chance. On my knees, I reached for the gun, but he slammed me against the door of the car. My head hit the glass and smashed it. But the gun was in my hand. He tried to secure my hand, but I pulled it free and released three shots into his stomach. He grabbed his belly and began to breathe heavy. Then he fell forward toward me. I pushed him aside and he fell like a sack of dirt to the floor.

The side window of a *bodega* was in front of me, and the people inside were all pressing against the glass, trying to look out. Next to it, a Pakistani man in a candy-store window was staring at me. Several people had stopped to look, but kept a respectful distance. There was some blood running down from my left temple. I turned my attacker over and searched his pocket until I took out a heavy wallet. Inside the wallet was a police shield and a driver's license. I recognized the dead man as soon as I saw the name: Quinten Neferkara. What was missing were his glasses. I checked his breathing. He was dead.

A siren sounded down the street, and that was my cue to get out of there. There was a horrible feeling in my stomach. It was a feeling of doom, a lonely doom that didn't allow you to share it with anybody else. I wanted to run away and crawl into a deep hole where no one would find me, where I could ponder my disastrous fate, where I could better envision the cross that was laid on me. It was the first time I had ever killed a man, and not simply a man, but a police officer. It was done in self-defense; he wanted to kill me first, but who was going to believe me? I couldn't turn myself in. They'd either send me away for life or send someone else to kill me. There was little doubt now in my mind that the police were involved in Pepito's death. Perhaps they were afraid that in investigat-

Project Death: A Tito Rico Mystery

ing Pepito's murder, I was going to expose them. That was why they had to eliminate me.

I threw the gun under the car behind me and edged slowly away from the dead man, looking at the people, making sure that no one was going to try to stop me. When I was halfway down the block, I broke into a run and went up a side street. The street was an incline, and I was breathing hard by the time I had gone several blocks. I ran until I reached Grand Concourse, a wide street with large, imposing buildings to each side. The traffic was moving, and so I had to wait for the light to change, looking behind me in case I was being followed. As soon as the cars stopped, I crossed the street and ran until I reached the C train. Before I went into the station, I used a sheet of newspaper and some saliva to clean some of the blood off my face. I also took off my work-shirt and threw it into a garbage bin.

I rode back into Manhattan without a problem, except when the blood from my cut started dripping onto my white T-shirt. I hoped that nobody would notice, the way New Yorkers never notice anything and so therefore do not get involved. But an old, black lady became concerned and offered me a few tissues.

When I arrived back at the Claire View, I headed to the bathroom, but somebody was using it. I could tell by the smell what they were using it for. I went back to my room and lay down on the bed for a while, keeping my ears open for the flush. When whoever was in the bathroom was finished, I went in, held my breath and properly cleaned out my wound. It wasn't that bad of a cut, but there were bits of glass stuck in with the dried blood. I washed my face and stanched the remaining blood with some wet toilet tissue. I must have been in the bathroom a long time, because a woman knocked on the door and told me to hurry up. When I stepped out, a short, pregnant, coal-black woman was standing there. Her front teeth were grown on each other and her head was tied with a bandanna, as if she was doing housework. She was about to say something nasty when she looked up at my face.

"Where you stayin'?" she asked me in a gravel voice.

"Just visiting somebody," I said.

"If you want some company, I'm upstairs," she said, and smiled as sexy as someone with crooked can could smile. I walked to the stairs, as if I was going down, but then went into my room as soon as she had closed the bathroom door.

I had brought a few things that I thought I would need from my apartment: clothes, some non-perishable food and a transistor radio that had been in my family for years. I think it was the very first radio my father bought in this country after he arrived from Cuba. It was a General Electric AM radio, about the size of a shoe box, with two small knobs. There was more static than anything else, but I was able to tune it to a station that sounded fairly clear. That was where I left it, very low. I should have brought a fan with me also, because the room was hot, but I knew that I could not return to my apartment after what had happened. That would be the first place the cops would look.

Few people, especially blacks and Hispanics, like the police. All we think about is Rodney King and the countless other instances of racism and brutality. But when there's a problem, the police are the only thing most people have to protect them. So you can imagine what a hole you're in when even the police are against you.

CHAPTER FIFTEEN

Belinda Pagan was a girlfriend of mine in my younger days. Luckily, after we broke up, there were no hard feelings between us. We still stayed friends. That was because we still liked each other and would get together sometimes anyway. She was a small woman, tawny-colored, and always real conscious about the way she looked. Her nails were always long and red, her clothes just tight enough, her black hair done up in the latest street style. She worked at Columbia-Presbyterian as a nurse's assistant, checking in patients, bringing them food, making sure they took their medicine. The night I called her, I hadn't seen her in three years. But I guessed, from the sound of her high, excited voice, that she still looked much the same.

"Tito!, I don't believe it!" she screeched into the phone. "How are you, baby?"

"Pretty good, Belinda."

"It's been such a long time. Where you been, honey?"

"Same place as always," I said, wanting to cut the small talk. "Listen, I need a favor."

"What is it?"

"Did you hear about this guy, a black guy, that was admitted to the hospital a few days ago all cut up?"

"Honey," Belinda said with a laugh, "half the people in that hospital are black guys who got stabbed or shot."

"They found this guy in an abandoned lot off 125th Street. It was in the paper a few days ago."

"I work in the pediatric ward now, so I wouldn't have seen this guy anyway. He was a friend of yours?"

"Yeah."

There was a pause on Belinda's side.

"Why are you calling me, Tito?"

"I just want to know where he is."

"Just call the hospital. You don't have the number?"

"Actually, Belinda, I don't know him," I had to admit. "I don't even know his name. That's why I'm calling you. I need to talk with this guy."

"What's going on with you, Tito? Whatta you up to?"

"Nothing. Can you help me out?"

"Maybe."

"What you mean maybe?"

"If you promise to come by and see me tonight."

I was at a pay phone and I could hear clicking noises. I was waiting for the recording to tell me to deposit more money.

"Weren't you living with Andre?"

"I threw him out already."

"All right," I said. "I'll come and see you, but not tonight. I need you to get me this information first."

"When?"

"As soon as you can."

"No, I mean, when are you coming to see me?"

"Belinda, I don't know. Just get me this guy's name and where he is."

The recorded operator cut me off, asking me for more money.

"You promise?"

"Yes."

"All right, I'll see what I can do, honey. Give me your number."

"I don't have a phone right now. Can I call you tomorrow night? Will you have it by then?"

There was another long pause from Belinda.

"Tito, you involved in anything?" she asked, concern coloring her voice.

"I'll explain it sometime. Just get me that, okay?"

The operator disconnected me, but not before I heard Belinda say yeah.

⊰⊱ ⊰⊱ ⊰⊱

I went downtown to my bank and pulled out all of the money I had, about four g's. I knew that my account would eventually be seized if I continued on the run. But I had no choice. I was not going to jail until I had found out what happened to Pepo. Most of the money I taped under the bottom drawer of my dresser. The rest I kept on me.

The feeling of doom had still not left me, and so I went and did what every man does when he's very depressed. I bought a bottle of Southern Comfort, a six-pack of Seven-Up, and a six-pack of beer. Not having any glasses, I finished a beer and used the can to mix the hard liquor and the soda. I spent the rest of the day sitting on the floor in my room drinking, staring at a cigarette burn the size of a tea saucer on the torn-up, faded carpet. I learned to like Southern Comfort from a friend I had when I was working on my Associate's degree at City College. He was Romanian, or Hungarian, or something, and lived in one of the dormitories. He was one of the craziest white men I ever met. He was a genius, getting excellent grades in his engineering classes, but was totally crazy. He suffered from extreme depression, and the only way he could deal with it was by getting drunk every night. He would drink about six beers and a bottle of hard liquor a night. We would sit for hours in his room sometimes and drink, listening to his Grateful Dead collection. I never saw him happier than when he was drunk. He would literally yodel from his happiness. A man has to deal with the life he's dealt somehow.

I woke up the next morning with horses running around in my head. I shaved and took a quick shower in the curtainless tub of the bathroom. The floor was a pool of mud. The water was freezing, but I didn't mind because it woke me up. I decided to go see Mircea. It had been several weeks since I had spoken to her last. I wanted to tell her about what was happening before she found out the wrong way. The last thing I needed was to lose her.

My car was parked in front of my building, and that was where it had to stay. So I walked all the way to Broadway and took the train up. Since I had a couple of hundred dollars in my pocket, I stopped at a jewelry store and bought Mircea a gold bracelet.

Her brother José opened the door. He was taller than me, and thin.

"What's up, Tito?" he asked, looking past me several times down the hall.

"What's up, José? Mircea in?"

"Nah."

"Know where she is?"

"I don't know."

He was about to close the door. I put out my hand and kept it from closing.

"What's up, man?" I asked.

I heard Mrs. Corteza in the background. Her heavy steps sounded until she reached the door, pushed José aside, and pulled it open.

"Tito!" she said in Spanish in a tearful voice. "Why have you not come by or called?"

She pulled me into the house by my shirt.

"Mrs. Corteza, where's Mircea?"

"I do not know what has gotten into that girl! I have talked to her, pleaded with her, and nothing!"

"What'd she do?" I asked, concerned.

"She is seeing this, this hoodlum!" Mrs. Corteza said, and turned away.

I turned to José.

"What?" I asked José, who was looking at me absent-mindedly.

"I don't know, man," he said. "She's been seeing this guy."

Mrs. Corteza had gone into the kitchen. She liked me and didn't want to see me get hurt.

"Where is she?"

"She said she was going to the park," José said, and looked back into his apartment. "Come in, Tito."

"No," I said, and left him at the door. When I reached the stairs, he had shut the door.

The information I had just received had not fully registered in my brain. I left the building and walked calmly toward Riverside Park, keeping my eyes on clump of trees standing by the silvery expanse of the Hudson. The benches where I came into the park were empty, except for one with an old lady and her puppy. But there was a playground a block up, where Mircea and I would go sometimes. Even before I reached it, I could see Mircea sitting on a swing, on the lap of a big, dark-skinned Dominican with a thin, faded beard.

They both turned their heads as I approached, crunching the gravel under my shoes. Mircea took a sharp breath and stood on her feet. Her guy stood up slowly.

"Hi, Tito," she said bashfully, as if she didn't want her friend to hear.

I looked up at the Dominican, who looked me up and down.

"What you doing, Mircea?" I asked her, still looking at the Dominican.

"Tito, this is Crucito," she said.

"Let's go," I said, and held out my hand for her.

Crucito stepped forward like he was about to do something. I stepped back, took out my gun from under my shirt and pointed it at his head. Mircea gasped.

"Why you do this to me?" I asked Mircea.

"Yo, man, I don't love her that much," Crucito pleaded, showing me his palms. "You can have her."

"Shut up!" I said to Crucito, and then asked Mircea again, "Why you do this to me?"

Project Death: A Tito Rico Mystery

Mircea looked at me for a long time and I could see fire ignite in her eyes.

"I'm always doing something to you, Tito. You're the one who can't be hurt," she said sarcastically. "Maybe I should ask you where've you been for the past three weeks? Tell me, Tito. That's how much you love me? I'm tired of it, tired of your shit. I'm just a little *puta* to you, that you get with whenever you're in the neighborhood, when it's convenient. You never give a damn about what I feel."

She crossed her arms and her "attitude" became worse.

"You think you're a big man with that gun? Go ahead, Tito, do something! Let's see if your *cojones* are as large as I remember them."

Crucito gave Mircea a horrified expression. He waved his hands at me and began stepping back.

"Mircea, we gotta talk."

"I ain't got nothing to say to you. I never want to see you again in my life."

Hearing those angry words come out of her mouth made me feel as if somebody had swung a plank against my face. For a second, I thought of pulling the trigger on Crucito, although I really didn't feel any rancor against him. I had killed a man already, so another one wouldn't have made much of a difference. But I put the gun into my belt under my shirt and walked away without looking back.

⇒⇒⇒

I threw the wrapped box containing the bracelet I had bought for Mircea out of the window of my little room at the hotel. There was a third of the Southern Comfort left and two beers. I drank the liquor first, straight from the bottle in large gulps until I was gasping for breath and clutching at my burning throat. Then I chased it with the two beers. The last thing I remember was spinning the empty liquor bottle, imagining I was playing spin the bottle with Mircea. I wanted to kiss her bad, but the bottle never stopped to point in her direction.

CHAPTER SIXTEEN

It was the next night when I woke up, and it took me a while to realize it. My mood had improved, but I felt hungry and wasted. I went to Sylvia's on the corner and had smothered chicken, sweet corn, candied yams and a piece of lemon meringue pie. Then I called Belinda. She told me that a man named Curtis Hale was admitted to the emergency room with multiple stab wounds three days before. He was presently in a restricted area of the Critical Unit.

I suspected Curtis was dealing drugs, like Pepito, and would be able to tell me who had attacked him and why. It might have been the same person who killed Pepito. I kept thinking that a couple of corrupt cops were behind the murders, officers who were preying off drug dealers and gleaning profits or extorting, as the incident at Dixie's Lounge had made evident. That was my gut feeling, but I had to find out specifics.

Columbia-Presbyterian was on Broadway and 168th Street, not far from where I lived. It's a city hospital, and a training hospital, so it has had a bad reputation for a long time. But I was born all right in it, so it couldn't have been all that bad.

The main hospital covers an entire block. On one end is the babies', hospital, where I guessed Belinda worked; at the other, the Emergency entrance, and in the middle a main entrance, made all of glass and with a facade rising high like the steeple of a church. This part looked like it was built, or re-built, recently. The two ends were still the old building, of weathered stone and marble. I thought that I could somehow walk right in through the main entrance, but was stopped by a female guard sitting behind the center of a very long desk.

"Yes, may I help you?" she asked me, raising her eyebrows. She was a short Hispanic woman, looking about forty, with long black hair. She looked a little like my mother.

"I'm looking for Rodríguez," I said, using a very generic Latino family name.

"Is that his first name?" she asked, glancing down at her book.

"No, last name."

"What's his first name?"

"Juan," I said, using a common name. I knew there had to be a Juan Rodriguez somewhere in the hospital.

The guard searched her book, then she searched the computer. I was worried that the name wouldn't come up.

"When was he admitted?"

"I'm not sure."

She scrolled through her computer again.

"I'm sorry, sir," she said, "but I can't find this person. Are you sure he's here?"

"Maybe he's not, thanks," I said, knowing this way was fruitless. I went back out and around the corner to the emergency entrance. It was the same story. A guard wanted to know who I was visiting. I went outside again, exasperated. Belinda told me Curtis was in a restricted area and was not allowed any visitors, so it would have been useless to say I wanted to see him.

The only entrance left that I knew of was the one into the babies', hospital. I went through the door and saw two desks, one with a guard and another, across from it, with a receptionist. Two women, one holding a baby, entered behind me and I held the door for them. Without looking at either the guard or the receptionist, I held my breath and walked alongside the women as they passed both desks and entered a long hallway. I was waiting to hear an "Excuse me, sir!" from somewhere, but none came. I continued walking slightly behind the women until we reached a bank of elevators, where the women stopped to wait. I stopped an orderly with an armful of blankets and asked him if he knew where the Critical Unit was. He told me I was in the wrong building and guided me to the right place with a complex set of instructions.

I tried to remember the orderly's instructions as best as possible, took an elevator up to a certain floor, walked to another elevator, took that to another floor, made some rights and lefts. I crossed a glass bridge over 168th Street into another building, took another elevator, and finally reached a set of large double doors that led into the Critical Unit, with the words "No Unauthorized Admittance" in large red letters above it.

I retraced some of my steps and went to a family waiting room on another floor. I sat down next to a man in a hospital gown and with a cast on his leg and thought out what I was going to do. I couldn't go to see Curtis in street clothes; I'd be questioned in a moment.

A young orderly came into the room and gave a blanket to the man next to me. He was about to step out when I called him and asked him to bring a blanket for my mother. He looked around me, trying to locate my mother, shrugged his shoulders, and said he would be back in a moment. As soon as he stepped out of the room, I left my seat and followed him down the hall to a door. He opened it and searched into what seemed like a supply closet. Standing behind him, I turned my back and read some notices behind a glass-enclosed bulletin board. When he had found the blanket, and was on his way back to the waiting room, I went to the closet, opened it, turned on the light, and gave a quick look-over to what was available. Quickly, I grabbed some green scrub clothes and shot down the hall in another direction.

I found a bathroom, went into one of the stalls, and put on the scrub clothes over mine. After I left the stall, I went to the mirror to see if I looked convincing. A man washing his hands at the sink glanced at me through the mirror and went back to what he was doing.

══ ══ ══

Beyond the door to the Critical Unit was a wide, noisy hallway, crossed by another wide hallway, with a large nurses' station in the center. Doors to each side opened up to offices and patients' rooms. Doctors in white and gray frocks and nurses were busy walking around, going in and out of rooms. A man on a gurney was quickly wheeled from one room, down the hall, and into another, while two nurses followed behind with the I.V. and other machines that were hooked up to the man.

A wheelchair, folded up, was standing by the door of an office. I straightened it out and pushed it down the hall toward the center of the floor. Near the nurses' station, I stopped, and looked around at the four hallways. At the end of the one on my left was another set of double doors. A small, young, Filipino nurse came from behind the nurses' station with a clipboard under her arm. As she was about to pass by me, I stopped her.

"Which wing is restricted now?" I asked, with an honest smile.

The nurse smiled, too.

"The same as always," she said, and pointed to the hallway with the double doors.

"Thanks," I said, and pushed the chair toward the double doors. These led into another, quieter hallway which was empty of bustling doctors and nurses. I could hear the beeps of medical machines keeping people alive. The rooms all contained patients and were identified with the names of the patients written on plaques by each door. I pushed the wheelchair slowly, glancing at each name. There was one door without a name, but I passed that one and went to the end of the hall without having found Curtis. I went back to the door without a name, left the wheelchair parked outside, and went in.

Curtis Hale, whom I identified by his stat sheet at the foot of his bed, was lying on a raised bed with half a dozen tubes running into his body. His bare arms were covered in bandages, and a plastic mask over his face gave him oxygen to breathe. He was young and muscular, with blotched, brown skin, a closely shaved head, and a pierced left ear. His eyes were closed and his mouth and nose were ringed with a white crust. There were other life-support machines in one corner of the room, as well as closets and cabinets filled with medical instruments and supplies, in case they had to work on him right there in the room.

Every time Curtis took a breath, he fogged up the inside of his mask. I watched him for a minute or two, afraid of disturbing him. But I had made it that far and had to question him.

"Curtis?" I whispered.

I said his name a few more times, and nudged his arm. He opened a pair of yellow eyes slowly, and turned his head to look at me. His eyes scanned me from bottom to top.

"Curtis, my name's Tito Rico. I read what happened to you in the paper, and I'm real sorry. I hope you make it all right, man."

Curtis moved his mouth to speak, but no sound came out.

"I need to know who did this to you," I said, coming closer. "I'm not the police, so you don't have to worry."

Curtis coughed and fogged up his mask. He cleared his throat several times and then pulled down the mask.

"I tol' 'em all that happen'd," he said in a raspy, tired, voice.

"You told the police?"

He nodded his head.

"Like I said, I'm not the police. A friend of mine was killed in the projects last month. I've been trying to find out what's going on. Tell me what happened to you."

Project Death: A Tito Rico Mystery

"Got jumped, man. Guys tried to rob me."

"Who?"

"I don't know, man."

"Curtis, listen to me. People have been getting killed and attacked at those projects. My friend was dealing. Another guy who got killed was dealing or using. When I read about you in the paper, I told myself that was what you were doing, too. I'm not going to hurt you. Like I said, I'm not the police. I'm just a guy like you. I know you weren't mugged. I think you know who did this to you, but you're not saying."

Curtis shook his head. He raised his arm slowly and reached for a buzzer on a wire that hung by his head. I pulled it away from his reach.

"Curtis, you gotta tell me!"

"They'll kill me, man!"

"Who'll kill you? Who?"

Curtis didn't answer. Instead his eyes looked beyond me to the door. I turned to see the Filipino nurse. She was standing at the door with her arms crossed.

"Excuse me," she said, "what are you doing in here?"

"I, I was just checking on the patient."

"You have no reason to be in here."

She came to the bed and put the mask back over Curtis' mouth and nose.

"Why are you in here? You don't work in this wing."

I began to inch toward the door. The nurse looked down at my chest .

"Where's your identification?"

"Just take it easy," I said.

She turned back to Curtis to make sure he was all right. Then she walked toward the door, but making a wide circle around me.

"You stay right there," she said sternly, keeping her two slit eyes coldly on me. As soon as she stepped out, she began to run down the hall screaming, "Call security! Somebody call security!"

I glanced at Curtis again and ran after her until she reached the double doors. Then I stopped and looked back to the other end of the hallway, where there was a window. Next to the window was an exit. I ran toward the exit, and as I entered the stairwell, heard the double doors open, followed by a number of agitated voices. I ran down the stairs for several flights, and then came out onto an empty floor of various medical departments. I ran from there into another area that seemed like a child care-center, where I slowed down to a walk. Small children played in large, colorful, padded rooms. The only way out, apart from the direction I had come, was a locked door and an elevator. When the elevator arrived, I got on with an Oriental doctor and a smelly old Orthodox Jew with a long, yellowed beard and a dusty three-piece suit. I pressed the first floor and tried hard to control my heavy breathing. The doctor left the elevator on the fourth floor, and several more people got on. When the doors opened again, on the first floor, a large group of people pressed around the elevator as we tried to squeeze out.

A dark, marbled atrium opened up in front of me, with an exit at the far end watched over by a guard at a desk. To my right was a corridor leading to Emergency. I could see several cops and brawny paramedics standing around.

Project Death: A Tito Rico Mystery

The atrium had a vaulted stone roof, a hard, polished floor, and a bronze bust of some philanthropist on a pedestal in the center. Hugging the walls were chairs and benches where people sat and waited. I walked slowly through the atrium, keeping my eyes on the hazy brightness of the daylight coming in through the revolving door. The guard at the door, a tall, thin, black man, looked at me and kept his eyes on me as I approached. My eyes met him once, but then I looked away. I just continued walking. I was past the bust of the philanthropist when footsteps resounded after me.

"That's him!" I heard behind me. I turned to see three cops and two security guards in white shirts. One of the cops had his radio in his hand and was talking into it. All five began to approach me, spreading out. I looked back toward the exit, and the guard had his radio at his ear. He left his desk and stood in front of the door, blocking the light with his tall frame.

"Don't move, mister!" one of the cops, a black female, yelled at me. Another cop pulled out his pistol. There was nothing for me to do but run toward the exit. As I did, the tall guard pulled out his nightstick and stepped forward, ready to swing. I rushed at him, and then went low into his belly. He swung his stick across the top of my head, and missed me. I drove him into the revolving door, causing it to spin, and to trap us momentarily before it opened to the outside. But I kept on driving the guard against the glass until I was able to jump free. As I did, one of the cops inside began to spin the door to reach me, and carried the tall guard back around into the building. That move gave me the time I needed to escape. I was running down 168th Street before one of my pursuers got outside.

As soon as I turned the corner of the building, I ripped off my scrub clothes and threw them under a parked car. Then I crossed the street and continued down into Riverside Park. I made my way into a large crowd that was watching a volleyball game, looking back occasionally to make sure I wasn't being followed.

I was safe for the moment. I had wasted my time at the hospital, but I was safe.

CHAPTER SEVENTEEN

I didn't make the first page of the *Daily News,* but they gave me a quarter of page four. The headline was "Another One of our Finest Killed." According to the story, off-duty Officer Quinten Neferkara, of Windsor, New York, a twelve-year veteran attached to the 27th Precinct, was shot and killed with his own service revolver by a white or Hispanic male in his late twenties or early thirties, about 5'10"and 170 pounds, in what seemed like a botched robbery attempt. According to witnesses, the officer was attacked from behind as he was descending the steps of the 176th Street station in the Highbridge section of the Bronx. A scuffle ensued, after which the attacker was able to get hold of the officer's gun. Officer Neferkara was pronounced dead at the scene from gunshot wounds to the lower abdomen. In an article that appeared two days later, as I expected, the white or Hispanic male was identified as Tito Rico, thirty-years old, of Manhattan. Rico was also a suspect in the murder of Wayne Edgar Jones of

Manhattan, and anyone with information should call 1-800-COP-SHOT.

I clipped both articles and tacked them to the chipped plaster wall of my room with chewing gum. I thought hard about how they found out it was me. It could have been that I left fingerprints on the gun. But I knew that whoever sent Neferkara to kill me obviously leaked my identity to the press.

A day after the second article appeared, I decided to call Detective Krieger at the precinct. I called him from a pay phone far away from where I was staying, just in case they decided to trace the line.

"He tried to kill me," I said to Krieger, trying to keep my voice low so that the man on the phone next to me wouldn't hear.

"Rico, where are you?" Krieger asked me. He sounded exasperated.

"You think I'm going to tell you?"

"You're wanted for the murder of a police officer, boy."

Had I been black, I would have been offended.

"Detective, the man tried to kill me. He knew what line I was working on, followed me, and tried to nail me. I don't know who these witnesses were who said that I attacked him from behind. He *attacked* me from behind. He was shooting at me."

"Rico, you're making it worse for yourself. . ."

"What the hell was he doing up there? Huh? Tell me."

"Rico, for your own good, tell me where you are. We'll send somebody over."

"Detective, you don't know what's going on. Those boys you got working the projects are no good. They're the ones doing the killing. They're the ones who killed Pepito. Now they're trying to kill me."

"What are you talking about, Rico?"

"They're trying to kill me because I'm investigating Pepito's murder. They think I'm going to uncover their business."

"What business?"

"I can't give you the details, but it involves drugs. And the way they're operating, it sounds like a lot of cash is involved. You better check out those boys you got working over there instead of coming after me."

There was silence for a few seconds. Krieger coughed several times.

"Why're you doing this, Rico?"

"Doing what?"

"You part of a gang? Tell me what gang. The Latin Kings?"

"I ain't part of no gang."

"None of this is necessary. If you just turn yourself in, it'll go much better for you."

"Listen, Detective, I'm about to hang up."

"Rico."

"What?"

"Listen to me."

I could hear a faint, irregular clicking on the line. I was being traced.

"I don't want to see you dead," Krieger said.

"Don't worry about me, Detective. I've been fighting people like you and what you represent all my life. I'll clear myself, you'll see."

There was another long pause, then: "Rico, are you religious?"

"Krieger, I'm not stupid enough to call you from where I'm hiding."

"Rico..."

I hung up the phone and called Jeri next.

"Hello?"

"Jeri, it's Tito."

"Oh, my! Tito! Where are you?"

"At a pay phone."

"Nearby?"

"No, not nearby."

"Is it true, Tito? Did you really kill that policeman?"

"That's not the whole story. I need to see you."

"Tito, you have to tell me what's happening. First the raid, and now this."

"Meet me at Grant's Tomb in an hour."

"Okay."

I hung up again. Next to Alonzo, Jeri was my only friend in the world.

➤➤➤

Whoever decided to put a mausoleum containing the body of President Ulysses S. Grant in Harlem must have been out of his mind. I've always wondered how many people up here knew who he was. My mother would take me to the park surrounding the mausoleum all the time when I was a kid. I ventured inside the tomb once, and on the tips of my toes peered down into the vault below that contained the two large black coffins, one for the president and the other, I guessed, for his wife. I asked my mother afterward who was buried there, and she couldn't tell me. Most of the other people who come to the park for barbecues, to play soccer or basketball, or just to sit and neck under the trees on the colorful, porcelain animal-shaped seats that surround the mausoleum probably don't know either. I admit I didn't know until I was in high school and took history. Then in my two years of college, I read up on it more. Perhaps it was appropriate that Grant was laid to rest in Harlem. He championed the cause of black soldiers during the Civil War. And I read somewhere that they turned the tide of the war.

Jeri, with little Paulette in a stroller, met me in front of the Tomb. We sat on the steps. She hugged me and gave me long kiss. But she was frightened. I hadn't shaved in a few days and my hair was disheveled. The strain of events was written on my face.

"Where are you staying?" she asked me.

"I don't want to tell you. But not far from you, relatively."

"I couldn't believe it when I saw your name in the paper. I was so scared for you. I kept on waiting for you to call."

"Has anybody questioned you?"

"No."

"Good. I want you out of this. If anybody does, for what-ever reason, you don't know me."

"Okay."

Paulette was holding out her hands for me. Jeri unbuck-led her and I took her up and sat her on my lap. She was a cute kid, with Jeri's wide face and small black eyes.

I wondered for a moment what it was like to be a father, to have a little life from God to take care of.

I explained to Jeri everything that had happened to me since Pepito came to see me that Saturday morning. She listened quietly, but with a surprised expression. When I was done, she took Paulette to her bosom and held her close.

"What you saw behind Dixie's, that had something to do with it?" she asked.

"That was the first time I started thinking the cops were involved. We got ourselves a couple of crooked cops, maybe more."

"I'm moving out of those projects."

"You'll be all right. You're not involved in drugs. Those cops are preying on drug dealers. For some reason, they're killing some of them, just like they killed my friend Pepito. It's too bad that guy in the hospital wouldn't talk. I don't blame him, though. They shot him up pretty bad. Probably would kill him next time."

"How long can you go on like this, Tito?"

"I don't know. I've held out this long, I can hold out some more. But I've got to clear myself. If I get caught, if they don't kill me, I'll get life for sure."

The bells of Riverside Church started peeling. I looked up at the massive building across the street from where we were.

"I don't know how many cops are involved. But Neferkara was from the 27th. I don't know how deep this goes."

"Tito, how can you go up against the police?"

"All I can do for now is run and stay alive."

Jeri put Paulette back in the stroller and then leaned against my shoulder, putting her arms around me.

"What happened with Dixie's?"

"It was closed for two days, but it's open now."

"You've gone back to sing?"

"I've tried, but Reedy doesn't want me back. He says its too dangerous for me."

"Where does Reedy stay?"

"In the same building, on the second floor."

"What do you know about Braxton?"

"The president of the Tenants' Association?"

"Yes, him."

"What do you mean?"

"What apartment does he live in?"

"Fifteen H, but rumor has it he doesn't really live there."

"How's that?"

"Well, people say he has an expensive house out in Long Island somewhere. They say he uses the apartment only as his office."

"Isn't that illegal?"

"I guess, but like I said, it's only a rumor. I haven't been there that long, so I don't know too much about it."

"You know where he works?"

"Not exactly, but I hear he's a lawyer or something. Something to do with the law."

"We got a man who looks like he's making big bucks pretending to live in the projects. Sounds strange, doesn't it?"

Jeri nodded her head. The bells were still ringing. If Jeri was right about Braxton not actually living in the projects, then it behooved me to investigate further, to pay a little visit to his vacant apartment. I remembered what happened when I tried to talk to him about Pepito at the meeting, and the trashing of my apartment a few days later. Braxton gave me a bad feeling.

"What can I do, Tito?"

"I told you I don't want you involved. You need any money?"

"No, I'm all right."

"But you're not singing anymore. Here's something."

I gave her three-hundred dollars. She refused the money, but I insisted until she took it.

"You got a baby to take care of."

"Tito," Jeri said to me, looking at me with eyes that were becoming watery. "I love you."

My eyes began to get watery, too, but I fought the tears back. I didn't feel so alone anymore. Jeri gave me something to hope for.

"I love you, too," I said, and kissed her tenderly.

CHAPTER EIGHTEEN

Alonzo and Hector met me at two in the morning the twenty-four hour McDonald's on Broadway across from the Sherman Houses. I had to give Hector twenty dollars for him to come down from the Bronx that late. He said he didn't mind helping, but to make him go out of his way was going to cost me. But I didn't mind. He was the best lock picker I'd ever seen.

We made our way to Pepito's building. With a baseball cap pulled low over my face, I sat on a bench with Hector outside while Alonzo went in and scoped the place. There were some kids playing in the playground. A radio was on the concrete near them tuned to a hip-hop reggae song. We kept our eyes on the door to the building. When Alonzo appeared again in the doorway, that was our cue to get in.

We took the isolated, piss-smelling steps all the way to the fifteenth floor. Both Hector and Alonzo, from their excess weight, were completely out of breath by the time we reached Braxton's apartment. While Hector regained his breath, I put my ear to Braxton's door and listened. There was no sound. He could have been home, and asleep, but if Jeri was right, the apartment was empty. It was a chance we had to take. Alonzo had his gun with him, and I had mine. If Braxton turned out to be home, we would have a much needed chat with him anyway.

Hector set his tool bag down by the door, reached in, took out what he needed for the first of the two locks, and got to work. Alonzo and I sat on the floor of the hallway with our backs to the wall, keeping our ears open. The dead silence of our corridor was interrupted only by the slight scraping of Hector's tools. Occasionally there were voices on other floors, the machine drone of the moving elevator, or the thud of a slamming door. We hoped the elevator would never stop on our floor.

A half-hour later, Hector had only the doorknob mechanism to pick. As he was working on that, on his knees, the elevator stopped on our floor. In the event of that happening, we all agreed to sit on the floor, as if we were hanging out, making sure we hid the tool bag with our legs. The elevator door opened and a tall, soot-black teen-ager, with lines criss-crossing his head and wearing a pair of black overalls peeked out. He looked at the floor number on the wall opposite the elevator. Then he snapped his head in our direction, as if he had suddenly noticed us. We all nodded our heads in greeting.

"I got the wrong floor!" he said with a grin, and got back in the elevator. The light from inside, reflecting on the opposite wall, moved up.

Hector wiped his forehead of sweat and continued to work. Alonzo wiped his whole face on the sleeve of his shirt.

Project Death: A Tito Rico Mystery

But it didn't do him any good. He was perpetually under a film of perspiration.

When Hector was finished, he turned the doorknob to show us it was picked. Alonzo and I pulled out our guns. Alonzo inched the door open slowly and stuck his head into the dark interior. He stepped in, I followed, and Hector followed me. Our eyes soon became accustomed to the dark, which wasn't entirely dark, because the windows of the apartment did not have curtains and allowed the lights of the city outside to enter.

"There ain't nobody here," Alonzo whispered. He reached along a wall for the light switch and flicked it up.

We were in the living room. A short hallway to our left led to two bedrooms, to a closet and to a bathroom. To our right was the kitchen. The living room contained a messy desk, various chairs, two small filing cabinets, a treadmill for exercise, and a cassette radio sitting on the windowsill. One of the bedrooms was entirely empty; the other contained numerous boxes of papers and files.

I went and sat down at the desk, first removing a blue paisley tie from the seat of the chair. I looked through some of the papers on the desk. Many of the documents pertained to the Tenants' Association, such as meeting minutes, proposals, budgets. There were also some legal documents, contracts, agreements, court orders. The filing cabinets contained files on various court cases. The files and documents in the boxes in the bedroom were of the same kind.

There was a picture of a small girl in a frame on the desk under some papers. The little girl looked about ten, chestnut-

colored, with a wide, gapped smile. It looked like an elemen-
tary school picture from the cheesy sky-like blue background.

I tried to open the top desk drawer, but it was locked.
Hector noticed it and made me move aside as he leaned in to
pick it. After a minute, he pulled the drawer open for me to
inspect. There were more papers, a pair of scissors, paper
clips, an empty box of pens, and about a dozen business cards
bearing Braxton's name. They were for a personal injury law
firm called "Mason, Turow, and Grisham." Braxton's title was
legal advisor. I put one of the cards in my pocket and closed
the drawer. The top side drawer contained nothing of interest,
but the bottom contained a Tec-9 automatic in a paper bag.
Alonzo took up the gun and inspected it.

"What's this lawyer-boy doing with a Tec-9?" he asked me,
handing me back the gun.

"Isn't that the favored weapon of drug dealers these
days?"

"Anything nine millimeter is what they like to use, like
mine, or like this one."

Hector, having wandered into the bathroom, called us
over. He was holding an empty red-topped crack vial between
his thumb and index finger.

"Where was it?" I asked.

"Down there," Hector said, pointing to the floor between
the sink and the toilet.

I went back to the desk and looked it over one more time.
I peeled back the various layers of paper carefully, so as to
leave it all as I had found it. Under a yellow legal pad was a
piece of yellow paper with various names and phone numbers
written in blue ink. There were ten names, first initial and
last name, and Q. Neferkara was one of them. At the bottom

of the list was a phone number with a 914 area code but without a corresponding name. I extracted the legal pad, ripped a page from the middle, and carefully copied down the names and numbers.

"What you got, Tito?" Alonzo asked me.

"Looks like a list of the cops working this turf."

When I was finished, I put the pad back where I found it. Hector locked the drawers with a turn of a key-like metal stub. I put the tie back on the chair and stepped back to make sure everything looked undisturbed.

Then the phone rang.

The sound startled us all who were trying to maintain the silence of the wee-hours. The phone was in the kitchen, connected to an answering machine. It rang four times until the answering machine kicked in.

"Leave a message," Braxton's hurried, gruff voice sounded. Then a beep.

A woman with, a sleepy, sensual voice talked to the machine. "Hi-i-i-i, Carl, it's Jewel—as if you haven't guessed —it's three-thirty in the morning and I can't sleep. Thinking of you. Thinking of last night. Call me as soon as you get in— all right? In case you lost the number, it's 555-8732. I'll be waiting."

She hung up. The machine clicked and rewound.

"What was that number again?" I asked out loud.

Hector repeated it, and I wrote it down with the name Jewel, Braxton's girlfriend. From the picture of the ten-year-old girl, I guessed that Braxton was a married man. He certainly couldn't give his girlies his home or work number.

We left the apartment and Hector relocked all the locks. Again we took the stairs down, but we did it slowly, stopping to rest every few flights. Hector and Alonzo stepped out onto the first floor first to make sure it was clear. I followed. We made our way back to Broadway, where Hector left us to go back home to the Bronx. He had to be at work at eight the next morning. We thanked him for his help and told him we would let him know when we needed him again. Hector was beginning to like what we were doing. He was excited about it all.

"So whatta we going to do? Use some of the evidence you found and turn Braxton in?" Alonzo asked me, somewhat disappointed.

"No, not yet. We really don't have anything yet. All we know is that Braxton and ten crooked cops are working the drug business over here."

"You think he killed Pepito?"

"Maybe him, maybe one of the cops."

"I say you just let me cap him. You know where he works, right? We can go down there..."

"Not yet. We've got to have a talk with my friend Noel first."

We took a cab to my place, and then Alonzo continued on to his. When I got into my room, it was a quarter past four. I could hear a creaking bed and muffled squeals and grunts from upstairs. Somebody was getting quite a workout. But I was too tired to care. I went to sleep and dreamt of pigs.

CHAPTER NINETEEN

Delroy Watts drove Alonzo and me around in his cab for two days as we tried to spot Noel. Delroy was a friend of Alonzo's, a large, quiet, almond-colored man with a gold-capped incisor. The whole time we were in his car, he said less than ten words. Alonzo would tell him something, and he would make a "Mmmm" sound without taking his eyes off the road. Alonzo told me Delroy had a butcher knife under his seat, and that he could kill a man without saying a word.

"Has he ever killed anybody?" I asked Alonzo quietly from the back seat.

"Why don't you ask him?" Alonzo said with a cruel gleam in his eye. "Delroy, Tito wants to know if you ever killed anybody."

Delroy squinted his eyes at me through his rearview mirror and made that "Mmmm" sound. I took that as a yes.

On the second day of surveillance, in the afternoon, I spotted a black Nissan Altima, the same car Noel had when I first saw him, in front of a *bodega* on Amsterdam Avenue. We parked across the street and kept watch. After ten minutes,

Noel and a girl came out of the *bodega*. The girl was holding a paper bag into which Noel put his hand and took out a can. The girl leaned against the Nissan while Noel drank his beverage and talked to her. She seemed somewhat upset, and kept her head turned away from him down the street as he seemed to be pleading with her. After five minutes, he crushed the can and threw it on the ground. The girl walked to the other side of the car and got in. Noel got into the driver's seat and drove off.

Delroy followed the car down the street, right onto 125th Street, then right down 3rd Avenue until 106th Street, the heart of Spanish Harlem. He double parked in front of a dull-red apartment building with a partly demolished front entrance. The concrete steps leading to the doorway were cracked with large fissures, and the door itself was dangling off one hinge. Three men sat on the steps drinking out of paper bags. Some kids were playing stickball in the middle of the street.

Delroy double-parked his cab several cars down. Then we sat and waited, watching Noel and the girl having a discussion through the partly tinted rear window of his car. After having some kisses forced on her several times, the girl made to get out of the car. At the same time, Alonzo and I started toward the car, Alonzo walking on the sidewalk and I on the street along the right side of the parked cars.

I reached Noel's window first and looked in.

"Wassup, Noel? Long time no see."

Noel was startled and looked at me as if he was confused.

"What'ju doing, man?"

Alonzo, in the passenger window, caused him to jerk his head in the other direction. Alonzo had his Glock dangling into the car. I pulled out my pistol and put it next to Noel's head.

"Mind if we go for a ride?" I said, and told Noel to move to the seat next to him. I got into the driver's seat and Alonzo sat in the back.

"What'ju think you're doing, man?" Alonzo said, trying to sound tough. But I knew he was scared witless.

"Shut up!" Alonzo growled and lightly slapped Noel on the head with the side of his gun. "I'll kill you in a second if you don't shut up."

I waved to Delroy and waited until he drove past me. Then I started the Nissan and headed back smoothly to the West Side.

⟿⟿⟿

About fifteen years ago, a bar on the corner of 133rd and Broadway burned down after a customer was knifed in a dispute over a sports bet. The fire caused the building above the bar to be gutted. The bar was boarded up and the sidewalk around it torn up to discourage loitering. But as kids, we discovered a way into the condemned part of the building through a wood door in the back, which, though chained forever shut, acquired a brittleness from its scorching ordeal through the fire.

I parked the Nissan on 133rd and with Alonzo dragged Noel at gunpoint into the bar through the back door. The inside was a mess of burned wood were and plaster. Half the ceiling had caved in and beams of wood still hung suspended from above. A little bit of light came in through cracks in the boarded-up windows and from the windows in the upper levels. It all looked much the same as we remembered it.

The bar, its shiny veneer burned off, was still against one wall. Alonzo found a chair, put its back against the bar, and pushed Noel roughly down on it. With his gun hanging in his hand at his waist, he cleared off the debris from the top of the bar and leaned against it.

I put my gun into my belt and stood in front of Noel, whose fear had turned to anger. He looked at me maliciously. My voice echoed in the cavernous interior.

"The last time I saw you," I said, "you and your friends were after me, remember that?"

Noel nodded his head.

"I don't know what you thought, but like I told you, I'm not with the police. Never was and never will be. All I'm doing is trying to find out what happened to my friend Pepito. I think you know something, maybe even who killed him and why."

"I told ju I know not'ing."

"This motherfucka sound like he just got off the boat yesterday," Alonzo said.

"Noel, I know that there are cops involved. I know you're afraid of them, too. They seem to be running a big operation over there. They're killing drug dealers, guys like you. You could be next. Who knows? You cross them and you can end up like Pepito."

"I don't know who killed Pepito."

"Maybe you don't, but you do know what's going on in those projects."

"There ain't noting going on. Ju crazy."

"You're afraid, aren't you, Noel? You're afraid to talk. You know what'll happen to you if you do."

"I ain't afraid a 'not'ing."

"You know a guy called Curtis Hale?"

Noel's eyes widened.

"I went to see him in the hospital. He got shot up pretty bad. But he wouldn't talk, either."

I picked up a milk carton from the floor whose bottom end had been chewed away by an animal with sharp teeth. I held it close to Noel's eyes so he could see.

"If you don't talk to me, Noel, we're leaving you in here with the rats."

"Fuck you!" Noel said defiantly.

I glanced at Alonzo. From his pocket he took a pair of handcuffs. I took out my gun and pulled Noel up from the chair.

"What ju doing? Heh? What ju doing?" Noel kept on asking as I walked him to what used to be a restroom, only a toilet and some pipes remaining. Alonzo pushed him to his knees and handcuffed his hands behind him to a pipe.

"Ju can't leave me here, man! Ju can't!" Noel started pleading, but I was walking away. Alonzo took out a dirty bandanna and tied his mouth shut. I climbed out and Alonzo met me shortly.

"You think he'll be all right in there?" I asked him.

"Yeah, rats'll take care of him."

Alonzo laughed until he was sitting admiringly in the driver's seat of the Nissan. I had to remind him that we weren't going to have the car forever.

Dixie's Lounge was under a gray stucco four-story building with a small entrance between the lounge and the beauty salon next to it. The top floor was fronted by one big window and contained a real estate agency. The middle floors were for tenants. Reedy lived on the second floor, according to his mailbox, marked Telesford Reedy. There were about two dozen match-box-size mailboxes.

It was nine in the morning when Alonzo and me paid Reedy a visit. On the second floor we found eight apartments that had doors wide open. The building was broken up into single units. Each apartment contained four or five rooms. Reedy's room was next to a bathroom off a long and narrow hallway. I couldn't figure out why a man who owned a night club would live in such a humble dwelling. Perhaps he liked being close to his place of business.

I knocked several times on his door, but there was no answer. Alonzo was ready to leave when a series of locks began to click. Reedy, in striped pajama bottoms and a white T-shirt stained under the arms, opened the door and looked at me with reddened, bulging eyes. He opened the door further and I saw he had a small caliber gun at waist level pointed at my gut.

"Put it away, Pops," Alonzo said, moving next to me. "We just want to talk to you.

"Whut you want?"

"I'm Jeri's friend," I said. "The night of the raid, you told me to take Jeri home, remember?"

Project Death: A Tito Rico Mystery

Reedy nodded his head and lowered his gun. He opened his door wide to a single room containing a twin-sized bed under a curtained window, a clothes rack and a chair. The floor was cluttered with clothes and newspapers. A half-empty bottle of amber liquor was on the chair.

"Come on in," Reedy said.

We went in and the three of us would have been a fire hazard. There was hardly enough air to breath. Reedy took the bottle from off the chair and pointed at it for me to sit. Alonzo stood with his back to the door. Reedy sat on the bed, putting his gun next to him on his pillow.

"The night of the raid," I said, "you told me to get Jeri out of there. We slipped out the back and saw two cops beating up a dealer. One of the cops mentioned your name. Are you paying protection money to these cops?"

"You FBI or somethin?'"

"One of my friends was killed and I'm thinking it might have something to do with all this."

"You Jeri's friend?"

"Yeah."

"How's she?"

"She's all right."

Reedy scratched his head. "Dealers use mah place foh theah bizness. Ah cain't do nuthin' 'bout it neither. On th' one hand, they make me let them use mah place. What cain Ah do? Dealers control this whole dam' town. If Ah don't coop'rate, they'll shut me down. Then, on t'other hand, you got the police. Instead a catchin' the dealers and puttin' 'em b'hind bars wheah they b'long, they make me pay 'em so's they cain turn theah head. That's how it works. First they ask foah two hunred, then three hunred, now four hunred a week. When I said Ah wasn't goin'a pay, they bust mah place up. You seen it. Shut me down and fined me. Fined me five-thousand dollars. Ah tell yah, Ah should'a stayed down in Lusiana where Ah b'longed. This whole dam' town's crazy. A man cain't figure out what to do."

Reedy put his head in his hands and shook his head sorrowfully.

"All those cops that raided the place are in it?"

"No, jus' a few."

"How long has this been going on?"

"Three yeahs."

"What are the cops' names?"

"Ah cain't tell you that."

"Why not?"

"Then they'll really shut me down, maybe kill me. Ah'm more afeard o' the cops than o' the dealers."

"I'm trying to put an end to this, Reedy. Those same cops probably killed my friend. If you don't tell me, I can't do the job."

"All we want is names, Pops. You'll be safe once these cops are out of the way," Alonzo said.

"Ah'm afeard to tell yah."

"Come on, Pops," Alonzo said calmly.

"All right, all right. One a them's called Riveera, the other's Compri. He's the one they call 'Busador' in Spainish."

"You mean *Abusador*, the Abuser," I said.

"Tha's him. Then there's this Polish fellow, Ah fo'get his name. And another called Vaskiz. Them's the ones that come into mah place."

"That's all?"

"That's all Ah knowed."

"That's all we needed from you, Reedy, thanks."

Alonzo opened the door, allowing in a pleasant wave of fresh, much needed air. I stood up.

"We'll come back if we need anything else."

"Theah breakin' me."

We were halfway down the corridor when Reedy yelled:

"Take keer o' Jeri! She's a good lady."

I promised him I would.

⟫——⟫——⟫—

Back at the Claire View, I took out the yellow legal paper on which I had copied the list of names and numbers I had found in Braxton's apartment. There was a J. Compres, an E. Vasquez, and a Polish-sounding last name: C. Litwenusky. They all corresponded to the names Reedy had mentioned, although there was no Rivera. We now had a list of culprits. What was left was to find out who was behind their operation.

And, in the process, who killed Pepito.

CHAPTER TWENTY

We could hear Noel crying quietly, his whimperings echoing in the cavern of the burnt-out bar. It was the next day around the same time in the afternoon. Noel was leaning back against the toilet, his legs stretched out atop ash and rubble. I could tell that even Alonzo felt a little pity for the kid. He unlocked the handcuffs, untied the saliva-saturated bandanna and pulled Noel to sit on top of the toilet. Noel had wetted his pants and we could smell the pee. He sat on the toilet rubbing his wrists and trying to calm the last bit of tears.

"I guess he's afraid of the dark," Alonzo said to break the silence.

"You ready to talk?" I asked Noel, looking at him straight in the eyes.

"How could ju leab me here?!" Noel blurted in a last spasm of tearful emotion. Then he was calm.

"Tell me all you know," I said.

"Ju wont leave me here again?"

"Not if you talk."

"I don't know who killed Pepito."

"No, but you know why he was killed."

Noel glanced at Alonzo, who had his Glock visible in his belt.

"If dey find out, I'm dead."

"What? That you talked?"

"Yeah."

"We're not going to tell, I promise."

"Ju don't care not'ing about me."

"It's not you we're after, Noel."

"There are these cops, man. They control everything around here. Noting goes down without dem."

"What they do?"

"Dey beat up dealers, steal their drugs, and sell them to other dealers. Dey take protection money. Dey rob dealer's houses when dere's a bust, keep the money and drugs. All that shit."

"You've seen them do these things."

"Hell, yeah."

"What about you?"

"Not me. Dey don't do not'ing to me 'cause I help dem out. I sell dere drugs."

"What about others, like Pepito, or Curtis Hale?"

"Maybe dey didn't want to pay protection money or maybe dey say dey was going to report dem, I don't know. But all I know is that if ju don't do what dey say, dey kill ju."

"You know these cops' names?"

"Some of dem."

"Quinten Neferkara?"

"Yeah, we called him *El Prieto.*"

"Guys like Compres, Vásquez and Rivera?""

"Yeah, dey call José Compres *Abusador* 'cause he likes to beat ju up."

"These are all cops from the 27th?"

"Yeah, man."

"And Braxton's the boss?"

"He runs things. He's like the president."

"You part of a gang?"

"Yeah, Y.B.C."

"Young Bright Children?"

"Yeah."

"Any other gangs around there?"

"Yeah, man, a few. The Assassins, Power, the Latin Kings, D & L."

"D & L?"

"Yeah, Dark and Lovely."

"They're a Bronx gang," Alonzo said.

"Yeah, but dey sell to us sometimes. Dere's going to be a big sale soon."

"When?"

"Next week."

"What's selling?"

I think dey got some coke. We're getting it for two hundred."

"Where's it going to be?"

"Up in Hunt's Point."

"How much you going to sell it for?"

"A coupl'a mil."

"You buying?"

"Nah, Braxton's doing it himself. Den he give it to us to sell. Braxton's getting into dat, buying his own shit. Before, he never did dat."

"He's becoming a dealer himself?"

"Yeah, man."

I called Alonzo to me. He put his ear close, but kept his eyes on Noel.

"Should we let him go?" I asked him in a whisper.

"Not yet, we still might need him for something," Alonzo said after a moment of thought.

"You hungry?" I asked Noel.

"What ju tink?"

"We'll be back with some food."

Noel started to shout at me as Alonzo handcuffed him again, telling me I told him I was going to free him if he talked. He was shaking and raving, and I thought he was going to pull the pipe out of the floor.

Alonzo parked the car in front of a grocery store on 125th so that he could go in and get some food for Noel. I walked to a pay phone on the corner and called Krieger again at the precinct. The first time I called him, he sounded excited to hear my voice. This time he was irritated.

"Rico, you're playing games with me."

"Detective, you better call Internal Affairs and get them to check out your precinct."

"Rico, where are you?"

"Let's not go into that again, Krieger. And don't put a trace on the line. I won't be on that long. But I got a couple of names here you might know. I read the names from Braxton's list out one by one.

"Know these guys?" I asked.

"What are you up to, Rico?"

"Those are all cops from your precinct. Check them out, Detective. They're rotten. They're preying off dealers around here and making money. They're the ones who've been behind the murders, not me. Check it out, Detective."

"You're crazy, Rico. Those are all fine men."

"Follow them, put surveillance on them, do something."

"You can't run forever, Rico..."

I was about to hang up the phone when I felt something hard pressed into my side. I turned to curse whoever it was who had rudely elbowed me when my face almost hit a black man's brawny chest. I looked up into the face of one of Chimp's boys. He had a gun pressed into my left kidney.

"Come on," he said, and with a hand turned me toward the street, where a red Chevy was waiting with an open back door. Chimp, in an apricot suit and black shirt, was sitting in the back, patting the seat next to him. I glanced to where Noel's car was, but a van was parked in front of it and Alonzo still hadn't come out of the grocery store.

I got in next to Chimp, and the big man got in next to me. The car was small so I was pressed between the two of them. The other big man was the driver. The gun was still at my side.

"You shouldn'a lied to me, Tito Rico," Chimp said, his simian mouth so close to mine that I could smell sour alcohol on his breath. "You shouldn'a lied to me."

The car started moving.

"How's Alonzo Brown?"

"Surviving."

"You saved his ass, but you won't save yours."

"You thought I was going to tell you where he was?"

Chimp gave me a wide smile, but without showing any teeth. He took out a cigarette from his pocket, which his boy next to me lit for him.

Project Death: A Tito Rico Mystery

"I've been reading about you in the papers. Cop killer, huh?"

"How'd you know what was going to happen at Dixie's Lounge?"

"I know everything that goes down in this town."

"You know about those dirty cops?"

"Pigs play around in the same mud."

The car stopped by the desolate northern end of Morningside Park, an overgrown park that opens up like a chasm into a low-lying wilderness, the den of nighttime prostitutes, drug dealers and users. We all got out of the car, walked into the park, and down a long set of stone steps until we reached a grassy clearing surrounded by a rocky cliff face, tall elms, maples and impenetrable bushes. As I was going down, the thought of trying to run passed through my mind. But I didn't want to get a bullet in my back. The situation seemed hopeless for a moment, but then I got an idea.

Chimp's boy stood behind him, his arms crossed. I made a little distance between me and Chimp.

"I'm gonna give you one more chance," Chimp said. "I won't waste Rocky's time by having him rough you up, neither. Either you tell me where I can find your friend, or you're dying right here."

I stepped back another step.

"Chimp, how'd you like to make a hundred grand?"

"What?"

"A hundred-thousand dollars. I can get you a hundred-thousand dollars."

"You trying to trick me again?"

"I'm not. Listen. If you help me get a whole mess of money, I'll split it with you."

"Am I your bitch?"

"This is legit, I swear."

"Explain this shit to me."

"These cops are buying a load of coke from this Bronx gang called D & L up in Hunt's Point. They're paying two hundred grand. If I can arrange to change the meeting place, you can show up with some of your boys and say you're D & L."

"And then what?"

"We'll mix up some fake shit out of baking soda, but we'll put a few real decks on top so that when they check the load, they don't get suspicious."

"That's the craziest shit I've ever heard."

"I've seen it done in the movies. Nobody checks the whole load. And if they try, me and Alonzo'll be nearby and we'll blow some shots in the air. Everybody's going to duck and want to cut out."

"What if when you blow the shots, they think we got them set up?"

"You duck and draw, too. They won't know what's going on. We can split the money in half. A hundred for you and a hundred for me."

"This shit don't sound right."

"Two-hundred g's!"

"How I know you ain't tricking me again?"

"If I lead you to Alonzo, will you believe me? But you can't do anything to him. This money's going to be our peace."

Project Death: A Tito Rico Mystery

Chimp took out another cigarette, which he lit himself. He stared at me a moment, perhaps deciding whether he was going to go along with me or kill me instead.

"Take me to Alonzo Brown."

We climbed back up the stairs to the car. I was taking a gamble, but it was the only thing I could do to save not only my neck, but Alonzo's.

⟨＝⟩ ⟨＝⟩ ⟨＝⟩

I had a feeling Alonzo might have gone to the Claire View to wait for me to show up. When I saw Noel's car parked in front, I knew I was right. With Rocky behind us, Chimp and I climbed the steps to the second floor. Somebody was in the bathroom at the end of the hall, and we could hear the water running. The door to my room was partly open. I opened it slowly and saw a shirt on the bed.

Chimp followed me into the room and looked all around.

"Where's Alonzo?" Chimp asked me menacingly.

Rocky took one step into the room, when Alonzo came up behind him and clocked him in the head with the butt of his gun. Rocky stumbled forward and Alonzo jumped inside, grabbed him around his neck from behind, pulled him down on his knees, and pressed his Glock against his neck. Alonzo was in a white athletic shirt and water was dripping from his wet face.

"Tito, whut the fuck you doing?" Alonzo asked desperately and angrily.

I put one hand in front of Chimp and the other in front of Alonzo and the helpless Rocky. Alonzo was a foot shorter than

Rocky, but his powerful, muscular width made him formidable.

"Alonzo, put the gun away. They're not here after you. Put the gun away and let me explain."

Alonzo looked at me in a confused manner. He looked at Chimp.

"Tito. . ."

"I ain't playing, A."

Alonzo let go of Rocky and jumped back, gun ready. Rocky stood up and massaged the back of his head.

"There he is," I said to Chimp. "You in with us?"

Chimp put on a wide, toothless smile.

"Peace, my brother," he said to Alonzo, holding out his hand.

Alonzo looked more confused than ever. He didn't know whether to shoot Chimp, or me.

CHAPTER TWENTY-ONE

Alonzo wasn't fully convinced about the situation until, at Chimp's suggestion and with some of my money, Rocky went out and came back with his other big partner, Nelson, and enough liquor to keep us all drunk for a week. We sat around my little room drinking and hatching out a plan for getting our hands on this money. Once thoroughly inebriated, Alonzo and Chimp seemed like old friends and traded quips about the numbers business and the merits and downsides of jail life.

"Th'only thing's we gotta do's git a li'l muthafucka we gots tied up somewhere to git Braxton to meet you somewhere else," Alonzo said to Chimp.

"How you all gonna do that?" Chimp asked, and looked at me.

"I think he'll do it," I said. "We just gotta get some fear in him."

"Take Rocky 'n Nelson with you."

"Nah," I said, "Alonzo's all we need. That kid's already scared enough."

———————

"Noel," I said, trying to sound as menacing as possible, "listen to me very carefully. My friend here has been itching to kill somebody again for a long time. I can set him lose on you if you don't do as I say. When is this big sale going down, exactly?"

Alonzo had freed Noel's hands so he could eat the sandwich and drink the soda we had brought for him.

"Next Saturday."

"Who's going to be there beside D & L and Braxton?"

"I don't know. He used to go around with *El Prieto*. He'll have some of his boys dere to watch his back."

"I want you to tell Braxton D & L is going to meet him somewhere else."

"What?"

"You tell him D & L is not going to meet him at Hunt's Point but by Harlem River Drive on 125th. No, make that 135th, in the parking lot behind those projects facing the river. Eleven o'clock."

"Ju crazy, man."

"You do it, or you're dead."

"How da hell am I gonna do dat?"

"That ain't my problem. You figure it out."

"What ju going to do? Rob him?"

"You just make sure he's there and not at Hunt's Point Saturday night."

"But then he'll kill me, man!"

"He probably will, unless you disappear for a while. But my friend will kill you first if you don't do what I told you."

Project Death: A Tito Rico Mystery

"Oh, man," Noel said and stopped eating.

"I know you're afraid of those cops, Noel. You'd rather they not be over your head. They're not your friends. Maybe you're making a little money with them, but once they're through with you, they'll get rid of you. Remember, they may be crooked cops, but they're cops. They pretend to be your friends, but they're not. To save their necks they'll round you and your Y.B.C. in a minute and you won't be able to do a thing 'cause they're cops."

"All right, man," Noel said, "but where am I gonna go after I tell him?"

"Don't you got grandparents living somewhere?"

"Santo Domingo."

"How much's a plane ticket?"

"A coupl'a hundred dollars."

I peeled off four-hundred dollars for Noel out of my supply of money. Noel dropped what was left of his sandwich and stood up to take it. He pulled a wet pant leg from his skin.

"I can go?"

"Go ahead."

"What about my car?"

I nodded at Alonzo. He raised the side of his mouth at me in disapproval, reached into his pocket, took out the car keys, and tossed them to Noel. Noel caught them and walked out.

CHAPTER TWENTY-TWO

A series of housing projects face Harlem River Drive north of 125th Street, a complicated network of highways and ramps, and the four or five bridges that cross the Harlem River into the Bronx. If you live in one of those projects, you have a nice view of factories and other projects across the river, ugly buildings which in the early morning were clothed in an eerie mist.

At eleven o'clock on Saturday night, Alonzo and I climbed the steps to the roof of the southernmost building of the Horne housing project, the one that faced the river and had a metered parking lot across the street below, the place where the deal between Braxton and Chimp was to take place. The rusted door to the roof was so stiff that it looked like it was locked from outside, but a few kicks from Alonzo unjammed it. We went out across a ground teeming with crack vials and multicolored tops, used condoms, discarded clothes, beer bottles and crushed cans. Apparently, the roof had been a popular spot. We looked around, to make sure there was nobody hiding behind the large air vents or the tall ends of the elevator shafts.

The building was only twelve stories high, so it gave us a nice view of the well-lighted, empty street below. Alonzo brought a pair of binoculars with him. I took a look through them. They were powerful enough to enable me to read the plates on the cars below as well as the signs on the ramps and roadways that rose from the Drive like the strands of a cobweb.

We sat back against the low wall that edged the roof and waited. Every time we heard a car pass through the street below, we took a peek. At around five minutes to midnight, according to my watch, we heard a car stop, idle for a minute, and then become silent. We looked and it was Chimp's red Chevy. They parked in one of the parking spaces with the light on inside the car, but no one got out.

We leaned over the low wall and waited. Every car that came down the street, its lights sweeping the parked cars, we thought would stop. Five minutes went by. A car stopped, a woman got out and went into the building. Another five minutes. Most of the cars passed through the street on their way into one of the ramps. We began counting the cars. I was afraid Chimp and whoever else was in his car would leave. The light inside the Chevy went off. All was still. I tried to look into the car with the binoculars, but only saw dark forms occasionally move. Time was going by painfully slow. Every time I looked at my watch, it seemed that it read the same time from the last instance I looked. If Braxton didn't show up, then Noel betrayed us and Braxton would be on the lookout for me even more.

At ten minutes after midnight, two cars stopped by the curb in front of the building—a white Saab followed by a large gray Buick. Alonzo and I kept our eyes moving back and forth between the Chevy and these cars. For five minutes nothing happened. Then the Chevy started up, it's lights went on, drove out of the parking spot, and parked in front of the Saab, about a two car lengths. We saw Chimp's two big boys come out of the car at the same time as three men got out of the Buick. Then Chimp, in a mauve jacket and yellow pants, came out with a box and approached the Saab. Braxton left the passenger's seat of the Saab with a large paper bag. Chimp laid the box on the hood of the Saab, and Braxton put down his bag. A few words were exchanged and then Chimp, as we agreed, opened the box, took out one of the real decks, which we had put right on top of the pile, and gave it to Braxton. Alonzo had brought two decks of coke for two and a half grand. I used up the rest of my savings to get it. We placed the two real decks in the middle and the fake ones made up of baking soda, salt, and talcum powder—blended to have the consistency of real cocaine—underneath.

I held my breath, praying it was the real deck, as Braxton clipped open a blade, ripped the deck and dipped the tip of his knife into the power. He brought it to his tongue and tasted it like a drug connoisseur. He nodded, put that deck back in the box and took out a vial with a blue liquid with which he could test the quality of the drug. You had to sprinkle the powder in the liquid to see how red it got. The redder, the better. I thought Braxton was going to use the same open deck to test, but he reached into the box before Chimp could do something and grabbed another one. I was so involved in staring at what was happening with the binoculars that I didn't realize Alonzo was waiting for my signal. I wasn't sure if Braxton had taken a real deck or not, so I decided to act. Before Braxton could rip the deck, I nodded to Alonzo, who took out his Glock and blew some shots into the air. I heard confused yelling and saw another man, wearing a dark suit and with a white Panama hat obscuring his face, get out of the driver's seat of the Saab and yell back at the Buick. Chimp grabbed the cash sack and ran toward the Chevy. Braxton ducked into the Saab while the three men by the Buick took out guns. One of Chimps boys was trying to get into the Chevy while the other crouched beside it when Braxton's boys began shooting. Alonzo stood up, leaned over the low wall and with one hand started pumping out shots aimlessly at both sides. He had a maniacal expression on his face and the sweat that had pooled on his brow started dropping in all directions. I stood up and pulled Alonzo down as two shots came in our direction, one chipping concrete off the edge of the wall. I heard more shots and then somebody burned some tire and took off with a loud screech. Forgetting I could get my head blown off, I looked down again and saw the Buick starting up, taking off after the Chevy and nearly sideswiping the Saab. The man in the white hat got back into the car and drove off with Braxton. They all sped down the street for several blocks, went on to the highway, and disappeared in the sea of car lights.

Alonzo and me struggled to reopen the roof door, ran down the stairs, and out into the street. A couple of the decks were lying on the roadway, along with some blood. Somebody got shot, probably one of Chimp's boys. I started to wonder who the man in the hat was. He was white, I could tell from his hands and physique. Alonzo guessed he was one of the cops. The list I found at Braxton's place had two or three names that could have been those of white men.

I felt some water against my face. It began to drizzle, although there wasn't a cloud in the night sky.

"If Chimp gets away," Alonzo said, "we ain't gonna see a cent of that money. Damn."

"For our sake, I hope so."

"What you mean?"

"I'm thinking of paying Braxton a visit down at his office. I'll tell him I have the money, and if he wants it back, he's gonna have to come clean with what happened to Pepito. He's gonna have to tell me which of the cops killed him."

"What if he doesn't talk?"

"I think he'll talk. It looks like that man wearing the hat is the real boss here. It's probably his money and he's gonna want it back."

"Tito, that ain't gonna be enough."

"What?"

"We find out who killed Pepito, I take care of the sonofabitch. But everything stays the same. You're still gonna be wanted for murder. Braxton and the crooked cops are still gonna be operating. Nothing's gonna change."

"You saying we've gotta bring everything down?"

"That's right."

We got out of the street when cars started coming and the rain started to come down harder. I kept on thinking that it was going to rain so hard someday that all the bad things in the world would wash away. But it would have to rain pretty hard for that.

CHAPTER TWENTY-THREE

I laid low in my room for the weekend, listening to music on my little radio, drinking the alcohol left over from the little party we had with Chimp and reading newspapers. Alonzo was absolutely right. Finding Pepito's killer wasn't going to solve anything. Taking revenge was going to make matters worse for me, for even if we tracked the guy down and Alonzo did the killing, I was going to be pinned with the murder. What became a simple search for information had blown up into something unmanageable. I had uncovered corruption at the 27th Precinct that ran no one knew how deep. Even Detective Krieger, who I thought at first was somewhat sympathetic and on my side, wanted to nail me. I had no one higher than me to turn to. Everything I did had to be at my level, at the lowest level, when you don't have a good view of what is happening around you. Either I exposed the whole dirty game, or I was dead. I kept on hoping that by lying quietly on my bed, how to do this would somehow come to me. But the only thing that came to me was despair and a gnawing fear that I would have to flee the city as a fugitive and be tracked down by people who had seen me profiled on television's *America's Most Wanted.*

On Monday morning, I went up to my own neighborhood and picked up my car. Somebody had broken into my trunk and stolen my tools, my spare tire and battery, and a jack. I picked up Alonzo and then went down to see Braxton at the offices of Mason, Turow & Grisham. They were located on the eighteenth floor of a building with glossy, black windows four blocks west of Madison Square Garden. A strawberry-haired model who served as a receptionist met us as soon as we opened the door to the office. She looked up at us from a desk behind a high partition. On the wall behind her, the name of the firm was pinned up in gold letters. A man in a gray whalebone pattern suit was sitting in a waiting area next to the receptionist.

"Yes, may I help you?" the receptionist said without looking up at us immediately. When she did, her eyes widened. Alonzo was wearing a thin, black survival vest over a muscle shirt. I, unshaven, had on jeans and a black T-shirt. We didn't plan on looking so uncouth and menacing. We just didn't have any other clothes.

"We'd like to see Mr. Braxton," I said.

"Do you have an appointment?"

"No, we'd just like to see him for a few minutes."

"I'm sorry, but you need an appointment..."

Alonzo came to the partition, braced his arms against it and glowered at the woman.

"Where's his office?"

The woman's face became as ruddy as her hair. She swallowed hard and picked up her phone.

"I'm calling security..."

Project Death: A Tito Rico Mystery

Alonzo grabbed the receiver out of her hand and slammed it down on the cradle. The woman cried out in fright. At that moment, two doors in the office opened. A small, old man with a wrinkled face, but wearing a neat suit, peered out of one. Braxton, in a silver pindot suit, came out of another. He stared at us a moment, then took a few steps out of his office.

"It's all right, Phyllis. Mr. Rico, come in."

Alonzo was going to go in with me.

"Just you, Mr. Rico."

"Whut?!" Alonzo said, ready for a fight. I told him to stay outside. He sat down by the man in the whalebone suit.

I stepped into Braxton's office and closed the door. His window, occupying a whole wall, though tinted on the outside, had a crystal-clear view out from the inside. It faced another office building across the street. Braxton went to his desk and picked up the receiver which was lying on its side.

"Jewel, baby, I'll call you back. No, there's no problem. I'll call you back in a half-hour."

He hung up and sat on the corner of his desk.

"That was very nice," he said, "very nice."

"Two-hundred grand is a lot of money to be losing these days."

"Yes, my associate was very angry after what happened."

"Who's that? The white man in the white hat?"

"You sound like you didn't recognize him."

"Should I?"

"We want that money back."

"You can have it, as soon as you tell me who killed Pepito."

"You don't expect me to believe that it's going to be this simple. I tell you who killed your drug-dealing friend, and you return the money?"

"That's all I want. That's all I wanted from the beginning."

"You've made a lot of trouble for yourself, Mr. Rico. You should have left everything alone."

"That's the problem. As long as people leave things alone, shit like you and those cops are gonna thrive."

"You can't win."

"Tell me who killed Pepito, and you'll have your money."

"Tell me, Mr. Rico, how's that cute lady of yours, what's her name?"

"Who?" I said, my heart beating fast.

"That singer..."

"No..."

"Yes, the one you were speaking to when we first met. Jeri, that's it. Have you talked to her lately?"

"Braxton, if you did anything to her, I'll kill you."

"I knew you would come to see me eventually. The woman and her daughter are safe, for the moment. But that all depends on how you cooperate. We want that money tomorrow. If you deliver it, we'll return her to you. If not, she won't sing another note ever again."

I took out the gun from under my shirt.

"Put it away," Braxton said. "Killing me is not going to save her. Don't do anything stupid."

Braxton was five seconds away from having a bullet in his fat gut.

"Braxton, she better be all right."

"You give us back that money, and she'll be all right."

"Where?"

"Grant's Tomb, tomorrow night."

"You'll have Jeri and her daughter there?"

"We'll trade. The money for them both. But be there alone, without your friend."

I put my gun away and stepped out of the office. Alonzo stood up to meet me, but I didn't speak until we were in the elevator on our way down.

"He tell you?" Alonzo asked me.

"No."

"What happened?"

"They got Jeri. They want the money for Jeri."

"How did Baxton know you were with her?"

"He remembered me talking to her that night at the meeting. He must have questioned her later."

"Did you tell him we don't got the money?"

"No."

"Well, we ain't gonna find Chimp. I went by his place yesterday and it was closed down. You can bet he's gonna lie low for a while."

⫘ ⫘ ⫘

As soon as we got back to Harlem, I called Jeri. The phone rang and rang. I dialed again, hoping I had reached the wrong number, but still nobody picked up the phone. I kept on hanging up and dialing until Alonzo took the receiver from me, hung it up, and wouldn't let me touch it anymore.

"They're gonna kill her!" I swore to Alonzo.

"They ain't."

"Where we gonna get that money? Whatta we gonna do, hand them a shopping bag and tell them, 'There you go, the money, trust us, you don't have to check?'"

I was upset. I must have been crying a little because Alonzo grabbed me by the shoulders with two firm hands.

"Tito, don't bug out on me. Remember who's here. They won't lay a hand on your girl before I shoot it off. Just get hold of yourself."

The roller coaster of events since Pepito's death had caught up to me. Jeri was the only thing I had left. Jeri and her little girl. I tried to keep her out of my business from the start, and here she was, an unwilling pawn in this game. I wanted to go back to Braxton's office and kill him myself, but I knew that wasn't going to do any good. I imagined Jeri was chained up in some burnt-out bar like Noel had been. I kept on thinking of Braxton threatening her, and both my blood and my tears grew hot.

"I'll tell you what, let's you and me go to Roxanne's for something to eat," Alonzo said consolingly. "It's about lunch time anyway. We can think about what to do there. Roxanne's been asking about you all the time."

I declined, but Alonzo kept insisting. I told him I wanted to be alone for a while, that he could go ahead, that I would meet him later. Alonzo finally left me. I headed back to the Claire View, but then changed my mind. Instead, I headed to the Sherman projects. I was gambling on being seen in broad daylight by cops or gang members, but I didn't care. I remembered that Pepito was found dead on the tenth floor. When I checked the stairwell the day of his murder, I found a porter cleaning up the blood. Some blood, according to him, was outside the stairwell door, in the hallway leading to the living

Project Death: A Tito Rico Mystery

units. Since the blood was on each side of the door, it was most likely that Pepito was killed just outside the door, allowing the blood to seep under the door into the stairwell. Directly in front of the door to the stairwell was an apartment door, and there was a good chance that whoever lived in that apartment, upon hearing some commotion, went to look through the peephole. It seemed to me that a man getting attacked, with the purpose of having his neck slit, would put up some sort of verbal and physical resistance.

There was a police patrol car near one of the entrances to the projects off 125th, so I walked up to Broadway and went down Lasalle. Though there were many people, both in front and in the lobby of Pepito's building, no one paid me any mind as I went in and up the steps. On the wall of the third landing there was taped a white piece of paper with my name and a picture of me that was ten-years old, describing my crimes and asking for any information leading to my arrest. I found several more wanted posters on the other landings.

I reached the tenth floor and opened the metal stairwell door that directly faced an apartment marked 10G. After closing the door slowly, so as to keep it from slamming and making a loud noise, I rang the door bell of the apartment. Almost immediately I heard a "Hol' on!" from inside. Then someone looked through the peephole and regarded me for a moment before speaking.

"Yes?"

The voice was that of an elderly black woman.

"Ma'am, excuse me," I said. "I want to talk to you."

"Who you?"

"I don't know if you know Mrs. Espinoza. She lives here in the building. Her son, Pepito, was the one who got killed, right here, actually. I'm a friend of his."

The little light in the peephole grew dark and there was silence. I heard a shuffling.

"Ma'am please, I just want to ask you some questions."

There was silence. My mouth was near the door.

"Ma'am, I've been trying to find out what happened to my friend."

I heard her come near the door.

"I already talk to the po-lice," she said. "I don't know nuthin' 'bout it."

"I'm not with the police. Like I said, I just want to ask you some questions."

I put up my hands so that she, if she happened to look through the peephole, could see them.

"I'm not trying to rob you, ma'am. This ain't a trick. My friend was killed right here, in front of your door. I know you talked to the police."

I stepped back and put my back against the stairwell's door. A light appeared in the peephole. She was looking at me from the inside, and I was at a sufficient distance for her to see me completely through her door's fish-eye lens.

"I know you're afraid," I said. "I am, too."

The peephole went dark and the locks began to click. A cross section of the woman appeared as she opened the door as far as the chain would allow it.

"You killed that po-liceman," she said, keeping her large eyes locked on mine. Then she closed the door to unchain it, and opened it again. She looked out in each direction of the hallway, and then beckoned me to come in.

Project Death: A Tito Rico Mystery

"Come on in, quick," she said, and locked the door behind me. She was a big woman, my height, with a full wig of gray hair and very large breasts. But she had a likeable, smooth, brown face. I could tell that twenty years before she must have been a very beautiful and desirable woman.

She led me to a green vinyl-covered couch in the living room. Most of the furniture, including the large tabletop television, looked fifty-years old. The walls were covered with black and white photographs. A cage containing a small, red, chirping bird was suspended from the top of the open window. She sat across from me on a sofa covered with throw pillows.

"The cops was here askin' me all sorts of questions. But I tell them I didn' see nuthin' and I didn' hear nuthin'."

My eyes were attracted to a framed black and white picture on the coffee table beside me. I saw a beautiful brown woman sitting on a large rock by the beach. She was wearing a one-piece bathing suit, her breasts hardly contained inside, and a sheer white robe that flapped in the wind. I knew it was the same woman in a time when she was young and carefree.

"But I seen somethin'. There was no way I could'a not seen it with all the screamin'. It was the mos' blood-curdlin' scream I ever heard, worse 'n when my Pop used t'kill pigs on Sunday fo' dinner. Them pigs give a long, even squeal. But this scream I heard was high an' full o' pain. It almos' sets my hairs on end jus' thinkin' about it now."

"What did you do?"

"Well, I goes to the door, real quiet, and looks and I sees the backs of two men and one young man 'gainst the door out there. One man's got him pressed 'gainst the door like this...."

She pressed her forehead back with the palm of her hand.

"T'other's cuttin' away at his neck. It was the mos' horrible thing I'se ever seen. I only looked a sec, 'cause t'was so horrible. I ain't never seen so much blood coming from a man."

"Did you recognize the men who were doing this?" I asked, moving to the edge of my seat.

"Yes, sir, I knows both o' them."

"Who were they?"

"One was that po-liceman you killed."

"The other?"

"I didn' even tell the po-lice this, 'cause I knew they would'a come after me. I been so afraid they come after me. But I cain't hol' it in no mo'. T'other man live right here. Mr. Braxton's his name."

"Why did you let me in if you recognized me as the man who killed that cop?"

"Ev'rybody knows 'bout you here. But I knows Misses Spinoza, an' she tol' me all 'bout you, tellin' me you was a good boy. Anyhows, I knew what them cops was doin'. I sees 'em sometimes doin' bizness they ain't supposed to do. A lot o' people here know, but we's afraid. Who we gonna tell?"

"Thanks, Misses...?"

"Gillespie, Cristabelle Gillespie."

"Don't worry, Mrs. Gillespie, nobody knows I'm here."

"What you goin'a do, young man?"

"Pray for me, Mrs. Gillespie, pray for me."

I went to her and gave her a hug. She kissed me moistly on the cheek.

"I will," she said. "Jesus'll help you."

I left her apartment and ran down the steps, tearing down whatever reward fliers I saw. Keeping my head low, I walked out of the building.

Project Death: A Tito Rico Mystery

The proprietor of the Claire View was sitting behind his counter reading a newspaper. He looked about seventy, had a crooked spine that hunched him over, a large, toothless mouth, and a thin, irregular stubbled face that looked like scratched cowhide. He was wearing a blue and green flannel shirt buttoned at the thin wrists but unbuttoned to his stomach, the gray hairs of his chest visible. He was always behind the counter, morning or night, and had never said a word to me since I checked in, until I returned from seeing Mrs. Gillespie.

"Heah," he said, putting down his paper over the things that were on top of the counter. "Ah fohget yoh name."

I was about to automatically say "Tito" when I remembered I had checked in under a false name. But I couldn't remember it.

"Yankees playing tonight?" I asked.

"Yep, playing the Royals."

"How many games they out now?"

He turned a few pages of his paper and bent over to look at the stats.

"On'y three, looks like."

"Hope they win," I said, and began to climb the stairs.

"How you like yoh room?"

"It's great."

"Ah fohget yoh name," he said again, but I kept climbing and didn't answer. I became nervous at his sudden friendliness, but I had other things to worry about.

"You ain't got the money, Tito," I said to myself while lying on the bed. "Braxton's gonna want that money back and

you ain't got it. He's gonna have Jeri there, and he'll be wanting his drug money. What, you don't have it? Pow! Pow! In the
morning they find us all dead: Everything continues as before,
except that we're all dead, Jeri, little Paulette and me. There's
only one thing to do. I gotta save Jeri and her little girl. There
ain't nothing else. I don't care what happens to me anymore.
Whatever happens, even if Braxton gets caught, is I'm still
going to jail for killing that cop. I've got to kill them all. Whoever I see tomorrow night, I've got to kill. Just kill and kill
and kill. I'd never thought I'd get to this, but what am I gonna
do? Here's the money. Pow! Pow! I start killing. I'll kill like
Tony Montana did at the end of *Scarface*, when he was all
drugged up and standing on the balcony of his mansion with a
machine gun. He was shooting and killing like crazy, and getting shot, too, but he didn't care. All covered with blood, he
kept on killing. For Jeri I'll do it."

I felt the weight of the small gold crucifix I had carried on
a chain around my neck since I was a kid. It was less than an
inch long, but I could feel it against my chest. I could picture
the minuscule, almost indistinguishable Jesus lying on it.

"What would Jesus think? He wouldn't want you killing
like crazy. But, Jesus, don't they deserve it? I know you said
love and all that, but think what I would be doing. They're all
drug dealers. They're killing little children every day, every
time they sell crack or coke to some pregnant woman and the
woman has a kid who's born deformed or has seizures the rest
of his life. Good people live in fear of these people. Pepito was
dealing, but he didn't know what he was doing. He was a good
guy. You know how he took care of his mother and his sisters
after his father split. You remember that. So I would be doing
a good thing killing those scum. Maybe I'll go to hell, but so

what. At least I'll be saving people. I'll be saving Jeri and her little girl, and Mrs. Espinoza, and Mrs. Gillespie, and everybody else."

Somebody heavy was running up the stairs. I sat up on my bed. Somebody began knocking on my door.

"Tito!"

I let Alonzo in. He was out of breath.

"Word on the street's that Chimp's dead!"

"What?"

"Chimp, he's dead. They found him this morning in some alley in the Bronx."

"Where'd you hear this?"

"I went down by his way again. Couple of guys told me."

"That means Braxton got the money back."

"He got it."

"So it's all a trick. They just want to get rid of me."

"That's right."

"They plan to kill me tomorrow, maybe Jeri, too."

"She' gonna talk if they don't."

"Damn!" I said, and punched the wall, cracking more of the flaking plaster and paint.

"Tito, this shit is crazy."

The white man in the white hat kept coming to my mind. The overhead view from the roof was a poor vantage point for details. His face, anyway, was hidden by his hat. Braxton called him his associate, but it looked to me that he was over Braxton, that he was running the show.

I grabbed the yellow piece of paper with the names I had found in Braxton's apartment from the top of the dresser and looked over the names, trying to match the man in the white hat with a name. But nothing fit. At the bottom of the list was the unidentified phone number. I showed it to Alonzo.

"That ain't Brooklyn, Queens or Long Island," he said.

"I think area code 914 is Westchester. You got a quarter?"

We went out to a phone booth. The proprietor quietly kept his eyes on me and Alonzo as we went out.

I dialed the number. There were four or five rings and then a little girl cheerily answered.

"Hi!"

"Hello," I said, "who's this?"

"Meghan."

"Hi, Meghan, where are you?"

"In my house."

"Where do you live, Meghan?"

"In a house."

"Are you there alone?"

"Uh-uh."

"Who's there?"

"Mommy, Moses and Tiger."

"Who's your Mommy?"

"Mommy."

"What's her name?"

"Darla."

"What's your father's name?"

"Daddy."

"What does your Mommy call him?"

"Louis."

"Louis what?"

The little girl's voice was replaced by a woman's indignant voice.

"Who *is* this?"

"Hello, ma'am, sorry to disturb you. Is your husband home?"

"No, he's not. Who's this?"

"This is J.P Jones. I'm trying to reach your husband Louis."

"He's at work. You don't have his number there?"

"No, he only gave me his home phone."

"Oh," the woman said. "Hang on just a second and I'll get you the precinct number."

Precinct. She left the phone a moment then came back.

"Ready? He works in Manhattan..."

I took the number down.

"Thank you, ma'am, very much," I said, and hung up. Then to Alonzo, "He's a cop at the 27th. Got another quarter?"

I dialed again and waited. The name Louis sounded familiar for some reason.

"This is Louis Harrell, I'm not available at the moment, but if you please..."

I hung up the phone. Louis Harrell was the other detective with Krieger when I was taken down to the precinct to be questioned the second time. He was tall and athletically built, the same physique that the man in the white hat had.

"Alonzo, there's a detective at the top of all this. He grilled me with Krieger. Krieger may be involved, too."

We went back to the hotel. The old proprietor did not look up from behind his paper. I had not reached the top of the second-floor landing when I could see, through the balusters on my right side, that the door to my room was open a crack. I stopped and Alonzo stopped behind me. We both took out our guns and proceeded the rest of the way, stepping as lightly as possible, which did us no good because the wood floor creaked heavily.

Alonzo went past me and stood to one side of my door. We stood still a moment trying to listen. Then Alonzo, unexpectedly, kicked the door open and jumped in. I moved behind him in time to see Detective Krieger, who had been peering into the newspaper articles about me I had pinned to my wall, turn to us in sudden fright. He had his black horn-rimmed glasses in his hand and his blue suit jacket was lying on my bed. He was wearing a black leather shoulder holster with a long gun tucked under his arm.

There was a strange moment as Krieger looked at both of us and then at Alonzo's gun. Then he put up his hands.

"I ain't here to arrest you, Rico. I'm alone."

Alonzo still held the gun steady, but looked back at me for instructions. I went to Krieger and tried to pull out the gun from his holster.

"No, Rico," he said, and grabbed my wrist with a strong grip. "I told you I'm alone. Tell your friend to put his gun away or it'll be him I'll arrest."

I let go of the grip of Krieger's gun.

"Tito, what I do?" Alonzo asked me uneasily, as if being so close to a cop unnerved him.

"Why're you here, Krieger?"

"I just want to talk to you, Rico."

I told Alonzo everything was cool. He put his gun away and stepped outside. Krieger wiped the sweat from his brow and then blew his nose with a handkerchief he took out of his back pocket.

"How'd you find out where I was?"

Project Death: A Tito Rico Mystery

"You're a wanted man, Rico, don't you know? There's a reward out for you. Casey, the old fellow downstairs, called me this morning. Said he thought you were the guy I was looking for. Wanted some of the reward."

"That old bastard."

"Don't worry, Rico, you're not the man I'm looking for. You just sort of look like him."

"I don't understand, Krieger."

"We want your help, Rico. We want you to help us nab some dirty cops."

I had to laugh.

"Are you serious? First you blame me for Pepito's murder, then I'm a suspect when that other guy's found dead. I told you I killed that cop in self-defense and still you're after me. And now you want me to help you?"

"Rico, I have to act on what I know. I knew you weren't guilty of those murders, but what the hell else was I supposed to do? I've got to do my job, and if you're a suspect, you're a suspect."

"So what made you change your mind?"

"Well, I was surprised to find out that Internal Affairs had set up a little thing called Operation Checkmate a year ago to investigate allegations made by an informant that some fellow officers at the 27th were suspected of being involved in illegal activities. I.A. had kept it all a secret from the under-cover and anti-crime offices because they wanted to continue the operation for another year. I demanded to review the evidence already collected and was able to watch some interesting footage from a surveillance camera set up in a neighborhood store that captured an off-duty police officer apparently collecting protection money from a local dealer. After I saw that,

I knew there was something to what you were trying to tell me. So, Rico, before I go any further, let me apologize to you."

He didn't hold out his hand. He only looked at me and waited for me to say something. But I didn't.

"I threatened to let everybody know what I.A. was doing unless they began to tie everything up. They told me they needed more time and I told them I was going to get these crooks myself."

"You could start with your partner Harrell," I said, taking out the yellow paper from my pocket. "All these cops are involved. Look at that number down there. Recognize it?"

Krieger snatched the paper from my hand and looked at it a long time.

"That's Harrell's number. Detective Louis Harrell."

"Where'd you get this?"

"I broke into the apartment of one of the ringleaders, a guy called Carl Braxton."

"One of these men was the one caught on film. You've done quite a bit of work, Rico."

"No thanks to you."

"You sure about Harrell?"

"Ain't that his number there? I saw him, too. Him and Braxton were about to spend two-hundred grand on coke."

"What happened?"

"That ain't important. What's important's that he and Braxton kidnapped a girl called Jeri and her baby. They got her right now, and they're gonna kill her."

"What does she have to do with this?"

"They got her to get me. Like I told you, they've been trying to kill me. It's all a setup. They think I don't know what they got planned. They want to meet me tonight."

Krieger sat down on the bed, took out his handkerchief, and coughed in it.

"You've got to let me deal with this alone," I said.

"Are you joking?"

"You can't get involved, Krieger, 'cause you don't know who's good or bad at the precinct, and I can't let anything happen to Jeri and her baby. If you try to arrest Harrell or something, they're dead."

"What are you going to do?"

"That's my business."

"I can't leave it like this, Rico. Internal Affairs has enough evidence to put these scum away."

I had no choice. Krieger wanted to interfere. I took out my gun.

"What are you doing, Rico?"

I called Alonzo, and he came back into the room.

"Sorry, Krieger, but I can't trust you to help me, not yet."

I went for Krieger's gun again. I didn't think that at his age he could move so fast, but he shot up from the bed and laid a set of hard knuckles against my jaw. I fell back against the dresser. Krieger unclasped the tie from his holster and was pulling out his gun when Alonzo shot him. Krieger fell back on the bed grasping his left shoulder, blood beginning to seep down his shirt. As soon as I regained my senses, I went over and pulled out Krieger's gun. He didn't protest.

"You're crazy; you don't know what you're doing," Krieger said, breathing heavily.

I checked the wound. The bullet just grazed him, but he was bleeding generously. The real damage was to the wall behind Krieger, which had a hole three-inches wide.

"I shoot him bad?" Alonzo asked.

"We can't keep him here," I said. "That old bastard down-stairs'll turn us in. Can we take him to your place?"

Alonzo scratched his head in doubt, but then helped me pick up Krieger.

"Can you walk?" I asked Krieger.

"I can," Krieger said, bracing himself against Alonzo. "You're in serious trouble, Rico. Both of you."

"We'll take care of you, Detective."

I threw Krieger's jacket over his blood-soaked shoulder and stepped out. Two people down the hall were looking out of their doors. We walked downstairs and found the old man was gone, probably having taken off when he heard the gunshot. We got Krieger into my car and drove to Alonzo's place.

=== === ===

Roxanne was a tough one. She had probably seen many gunshot wounds in her life. Alonzo told her not to ask any questions, and so she got to cleaning Krieger's wound and bandaging it without a peep.

"What the hell are you going to do, Rico?" Krieger asked me.

"I've got to save Jeri, Detective. That's it."

"Rico, I don't understand you. You want justice, don't you? Taking matters into your own hands is not the way to do it. When these officers get arrested, you'll come out clean. You'll probably have to testify and answer to lesser charges, but you'll be acquitted, even of killing Neferkara. I promise you."

"I don't doubt you think that, but as long as they got Jeri, I can't do nothing else."

Krieger lay back on the couch, as if exhausted. Roxanne had crushed a couple of sleeping pills into some orange juice she gave him, and it was beginning to take effect. Moniqua, who had been playing in the kitchen, walked over to Krieger and showed him a black Barbie doll. Roxanne was going to carry her away when Krieger told her it was all right. He took the doll and studied it, and then handed it back to Moniqua, who was smiling gleefully.

"She's beautiful, looks like you," Krieger said. "What's your name?"

Moniqua climbed on the couch next to him. "Moneeekua."

"How old are you?"

Moniqua held out three, small black fingers.

"Beautiful child, miss," Krieger said to Roxanne, who came and took Moniqua away.

At six, Roxanne made dinner: baked chicken, okra gumbo, honeyed potatoes, rice and red beans. Krieger ate some sitting on the couch, the rest of us at the table. Then Roxanne took Moniqua into her bedroom, where Alonzo told her to stay the rest of the night. At nine, Alonzo found a leather bag, like the kind used to carry bowling balls, but big enough to carry two hundred grand if we had it. Then we filled it with dirt from Roxanne's plotted plants until it was heavy and bulging. Krieger watched us do this quietly.

"What are you going to do with me?" Krieger asked when we finished.

"We're going to take you somewhere," I said, "and leave you there. After that you're free to do your job. You've got the list."

"Don't you realize you're in enough trouble as it is? Let me go and we'll handle it."

"If there's one thing I've learned in my life, Krieger, it's not to rely on the police. Maybe down on Park Avenue you all 'Serve and Protect' and everybody loves you, but up here, you're as much a part of the problem as everything else. Maybe you give a damn, Krieger, but none of your other boys in blue do."

"And you," Krieger said to Alonzo, "I don't know who you are, but you're going along with this?"

Alonzo had not as yet said one word to Krieger. He did not answer.

"I don't care if these people you're after are the scum of the earth, you just can't murder them. You have no authority to do anything."

"It's justice, man," Alonzo said to Krieger for the first time. "Something none'a you all know anything about."

We walked Krieger downstairs, keeping our guns stuck into his kidneys. I probably would not have shot him if he had tried something, but Alonzo already showed him he wouldn't have hesitated.

I took the Willis Avenue bridge across the Harlem River into the South Bronx, Krieger guarded by Alonzo in the back seat. I stopped in a dark and desolate area of Hunt's Point, not far from Hoe Avenue where all the twenty-dollar prostitutes are—a wide, littered street surrounded by warehouses and factories. There were no people or traffic anywhere, not even a barking dog. The only light came from a single street lamp over us. The others up and down the street were burned out.

"This is it, Krieger," I said, getting out of the car, but leaving it running.

Krieger and Alonzo got out.

"Rico, you can't leave me here."

"Tell your boys to check out Grant's Tomb in about a half hour, at midnight. That's where I'll be."

Alonzo moved to the front passenger door, opened it, and was about to get in. I pulled out Krieger's gun from my belt and aimed it at him. I was taking a gamble because Alonzo was crazy enough to shoot me.

"You're staying, too, Alonzo."

"What you talking about, Tito?"

"I've got to do this alone," I said. Then to Krieger, "My friend hasn't had anything to do with this. Except for shooting you, which he did to protect me, he's clean."

"Tito, don't be playing like this," Alonzo said.

"I ain't playing, A. You've got to think of Roxanne and Moniqua. You've got a family now and you gotta stay out of jail."

"I'm gonna back you up!"

"Next time, A, next time."

I told them both to step away from the car. Krieger did, and, to my surprise, Alonzo did, too. I got in and drove away quickly. Alonzo ran after me, yelling out my name. When I was a block away, I threw Krieger's gun out of the window. All I had was my little .38.

⋙═⋙═⋙

The square plaza in front of Grant's tomb was lit by four lights on tall black posts. The American flag flapped in the river breeze from another pole. I parked the car on Riverside Drive under the shadow of the hill on which the mausoleum rested and I climbed a set of steps to the plaza. It was a few minutes to twelve. I looked around. There was no one in the

plaza or on the porch of the Tomb. There may have been someone hiding in the shadows of the six columns that stood in
front of the mausoleum, but I couldn't see into that darkness.
The only people around were a few lovers making out in the
dark recesses of the colorful and oddly-shaped seats that surrounded the Tomb.

With my bag in hand, I climbed up the steps to the Tomb
and sat on the top step, next to one of the columns and in
front of the two wrought-iron studded doors that guarded the
former president and first lady inside. There I waited and
viewed with suspicion anyone who appeared on or crossed the
plaza. When I saw a Saab park across the street in front of
Riverside Church, I tensed up and made sure my gun was in
my belt at an easily accessible place and position.

I stood up to watch Braxton get out of the car, followed by
Jeri holding Paulette, and finally a Hispanic man with short
black hair, sunglasses, and a goatee. They walked to the center of the plaza as I began descending the steps.

"You have the money, Rico?" Braxton asked

I came within two yards of them and threw the dirt-filled
bag in front of me on the concrete floor.

"Right here."

Jeri was holding a sleeping Paulette close, pressing the
child's head against her face. Her lips were trembling and
tears were coming out of her eyes. She was trying to mouth
something to me, but I couldn't make out what it was. The
Hispanic pushed her toward me and she glanced back at him
before beginning to walk toward me in small steps, as if she
was on a tightrope.

Braxton began to laugh cruelly. The Hispanic also began
to laugh.

"Finish it," Braxton said, and turned around. The Hispanic reached under his shirt behind him. I jumped forward, shoved Jeri aside with one hand, and pulled out my gun with the other. I fired twice in despair, without aiming, but the Hispanic fell to the ground and was still.

Braxton, who was walking away, turned around. Jeri was screaming. Paulette had awakened and was crying. Braxton put out his hands as I aimed the gun at him. The Saab started up and drove off. I could see a white man was driving, and it looked like Harrell.

"We can work this out, Rico," Braxton said calmly. "Name what you want."

I stepped closer.

"Why'd you kill Pepito?"

"He didn't want to cooperate."

"Why'd you kill him?"

"He owed us," Braxton said, his voice more anxious.

"How much? Five hundred dollars? You killed him for a fuckin five hundred dollars?"

My anger was so great that I pulled the trigger and snapped the gun forward, as if the added momentum would propel the bullet faster. But the gun just clicked. I pulled the trigger again and again. Braxton put his hands down and smiled. He reached into a pocket and unclasped a ten-inch Stilleto.

"Sorry, Rico, you should've let Compres kill you."

Braxton swung clumsily at my face and I ducked. While I was still down, I heard a shot go off behind me and saw Braxton stumble back. Another shot and he fell backward like a tree just cut.

Krieger was standing on the steps that led down to the Drive, the long barrel of his gun pointed and smoking. Alonzo appeared behind him, and then Delroy Watts. Alonzo ran to me.

"Tito," he said, out of breath, "you all right?"

"How'd you get down here so fast?"

"Delroy was around the way when we called up his company for a cab. He did ninety getting down here."

Delroy came up and checked the bodies. "Mmmm," he said, and that was all. Krieger, grasping his wounded shoulder, was the last to approach.

"Harrell was here," I told him. "He got away."

"Not for long," Krieger said. "Delroy, drive me to the station."

Delroy nodded and walked toward the steps, Krieger following. Jeri came to me and tried to hug me. With Paulette in the middle, we all embraced.

"Did they hurt you?"

"No, they just kept me in Braxton's empty apartment. Tito, I was so afraid they'd do something to the baby. I was afraid they'd hurt you."

"It's all over now," I said, and took Paulette securely in my arms.

CHAPTER TWENTY-FOUR

Thanks to Detective Krieger's testimony in court, I got off on all charges except possession of an unlicensed handgun. Harrell, thirteen cops from the 27th and five civilians were arrested on corruption charges and charged with murder, robbery, assault, tampering with evidence, possession of controlled substances, violation of civil rights, perjury, conspiracy and a dozen other crimes. It was the largest roundup ever done in the history of the New York City police, and the mayor formed a commission to investigate other precincts around the city. Alonzo got off clean, too. Krieger advised him to disappear for a while while all the investigations were going on.

Jeri and Paulette moved out of the projects and in with me. I promised her that as soon as I was able, we were going to move out of the neighborhood and to a nice part of Queens or Brooklyn.

I saw Alonzo one night at Nig's. He was as drunk as a skunk with two fortys down and one in the works.

"That 'tective wuz all right," he said to me, trying to keep his eyes open. "But wut we gonna do now?"

"What you mean?"

"I mean, we gotta do somethin', good or bad. We gotta get the posse back in action."

"Wasn't all that enough excitement for you, A?"

"Nah, nah. I did'n get t'plug nobody."

"Krieger took away your piece."

"I gots me 'nother one," he said, and pulled out another Glock from under his shirt and slammed it on the table. I quickly covered it with my hand.

"Put it away, A!"

He snatched it back and hid it under his shirt. I looked around. Nobody had noticed.

"You gotta stay out of trouble, A. You know?"

"Yeah."

"You gotta make sure your little girl survives all this shit."

"There ain't no muthafucka gonna hurt her. I'll cap his fuckin ass."

He was about to pull out his gun again when I leaned over the table and put a hand on his shoulder.

"I'll keep my eyes open, A. If anything comes up, I'll come looking for you. We'll be busting shit right and left."

Alonzo relaxed. He grinned and then smiled.

"See you later, man," I said. *"Cógelo suave."*

Alonzo put out his fist and I bumped it with mine. I left him and he was still smiling.

Project Death: A Tito Rico Mystery

⋐━ ⋐━ ⋐━

Jeri was sleeping when I got back to my apartment. Paulette was sitting in her crib playing quietly with a stuffed toy. I lay her down and tucked her in and told her to go to sleep. Jeri had an arm stretched out over my side of the bed and I got in and lay over it. Like a reflex, Jeri moved over to my side and held me with both arms. I expected her to say something, but she was still asleep.

Lying there in the quiet, it hit me again that nothing had really changed. Every time I visit Pepito's mother, I see dealers doing their business. I may have found Pepito's killers, but that was all I did. The good people still live in fear. Children still have to be careful where they play. I stay awake at night sometimes, wondering what else can be done. Then I think that I'm okay and that the people I love are okay, and I can finally fall asleep. But I know that I'm only fooling myself, and the next night I'm up wondering again.

The End.